Take me to your cabin

Her simple request set his body on fire all over again. He swept her into his arms and kissed her. Passion exploded as she molded her body into his, giving them each the closeness that they craved.

"I never knew how hungry I was until I met you," he whispered as the kiss ended and everything else began. He licked and nibbled and tasted her, relishing her neck and shoulders as his hands drifted to her breasts. Still, he wanted more. He wanted all of her. His body shook and tensed as his crotch began to throb with need.

She gasped, holding her breath and nearly exploding inside. A split second of nervousness needled through her. She hadn't done this in a while and never with a man she'd only known for a few days. But somehow it didn't matter about the length of time. In her heart she felt as if she'd known him all her life. She closed her eyes, letting the thick haze of desire surrounding them take her away. When she opened her eyes he was smiling at her. It was all the reassurance she needed. She looked deep into his penetrating gaze.

"Are you okay?" he asked softly.

She nodded.

"I want you so badly," he breathed into her ear.

"Then show me," she said breathlessly. "Show me."

Books by Celeste O. Norfleet

Kimani Romance

Sultry Storm
When It Feels So Right
Cross My Heart

Kimani TRU

Pushing Pause
She Said, She Said
Fast Forward

Kimani Arabesque

Love is for Keeps
Love After All
Following Love
When Love Calls
Love Me Now

CELESTE O. NORFLEET

is a native Philadelphian who has always been artistic, but now her creative imagination flows through the computer keys instead of a paint brush. She is a prolific writer for the Kimani Arabesque and Kimani Romance lines. Her romance novels, realistic with a touch of humor, depict strong, sexy characters with unpredictable plots and exciting storylines. With an impressive backlist, she continues to win rave reviews and critical praise for her sexy romances that scintillate as well as entertain. Celeste also lends her talent to the Kimani TRU young adult line. Her young adult novels are dramatic fiction, reflecting current issues facing African-American teens. Celeste lives in Virginia with her husband and two teens. You can contact her at conorfleet@aol.com or P.O. Box 7346, Woodbridge, VA 22195-7346 or visit her Web site at www.celesteonorfleet.com.

Celeste O. Norfleet

CROSS *my* HEART

™
KIMANI
ROMANCE

To Fate & Fortune

 KIMANI PRESS™

Recycling programs
for this product may
not exist in your area.

ISBN-13: 978-0-373-86162-0

CROSS MY HEART

Copyright © 2010 by Celeste O. Norfleet

www.kimanipress.com

Printed in U.S.A.

Dear Reader,

Thank you so much for your overwhelming support for my June 2009 release, *Sultry Storm.* Most of you wanted to know more about Natalia Coles and her anonymous sperm donor. In *Cross My Heart* you'll be reintroduced to Natalia and meet superstar Hollywood actor, David Montgomery—two people who share two very special gifts.

I got the idea from an article on in vitro fertilization and wanted to write about a woman who'd successfully undergone the process. I know you'll enjoy Natalia and David's story as much as I enjoyed writing it. If you want more updates on Stephen, Mia, Natalia and David, just e-mail me and let me know.

In the meantime, watch for my next Kimani Romance, *Flirting with Destiny,* coming out this winter. As always, I truly appreciate your support and will continue to write exciting, entertaining and sensuous romances.

You can contact me at conorfleet@aol.com.

Blessings & Peace,

Celeste O. Norfleet

Chapter 1

Unrecognized and unnoticed, David Montgomery had a plan when he walked into Nikita's Place. He placed a coffee and pastry order and then asked the clerk about the owner, Nikita Coles. She was next on the list, after her sister, Natalia. To his disappointment Nikita was busy in the kitchen and didn't have time to come out and meet the patrons. Thwarted, but ever resourceful, he grabbed a seat at a table in the rear with his coffee and newspaper and waited. She had to come out sometime.

He was angry, jet-lagged and exhausted, a dangerous combination. He had flown in from London two days before, and then he hit Chicago, Dallas and L.A., all in the span of forty-eight hours. So now, to stay focused and alert, he listened to the chatter around him. They were mostly trivial conversations about sports, cooking, current events and local gossip. He was beginning to think this was just another waste of time when to his surprise, after half an hour, a woman came from behind the counter with two cups and a small pastry plate. A few seconds later she was joined by a second woman. David sat and continued listening.

Natalia Coles's fiery dark eyes narrowed as she marched through the small parking area toward the main entrance of Nikita's Place, her sister's bakery and café. Usually low-key and calm, Natalia had a way of getting attention and getting her point across with little fuss. She didn't yell or scream or go in for high drama or disruptive behavior. Most days she pleasantly eased into her orderly life. Today wasn't one of those days. Today she stormed into the bakery like a hurricane on steroids. She quickly looked around, spotting her sister in the back.

"Over here," Nikita Coles called out.

Natalia nodded and smiled briefly, noting that her younger sister had cleared a table at the back of her café and waved her over. She sliced her way through the crowd and narrow seating, then finally reached the table already prepared with two cups of tea and a small tray of pastries. As soon as she got there her sister smiled and hugged her warmly. "Hey, girl, I wondered what happened to you. I thought you were going to stand me up or something. Come on. Have a seat. My break's almost over and the kitchen's been crazy busy all morning."

"You're not going to believe this. I can hardly believe it myself," Natalia began immediately.

"Whoa, calm down," Nikita soothed. "What's going on? You look exhausted."

"I am. I was up most of the night. You won't believe this. The city and state rejected my grant renewal applications. I was up half the night trying to figure out what to do next."

"Oh, no, Nat. I'm so sorry." Her sister opened her arms immediately. The two hugged. "I know how much getting that money meant to you."

She sat down next to her sister. "No, not to me, Nikita, to the kids. I don't know what I'm going to do now. The center's running on bare bones as it is, and I was really depending on the government money. Now it's too late to apply anywhere else."

"Do you know why or what happened?" Nikita asked.

"No, and I just don't understand it," Natalia complained. "I know I did everything exactly right. All the paperwork, everything was completed perfectly. I get that the competition is intense. The grants are amazing and they come with all kinds of incredible extras and benefits. They even include a summer camp option! I've applied the last three years and have always gotten approved. But this time it was different. I got a very polite 'Thanks, please apply again' letter." Natalia's voice cracked with emotion as she shook her head. "So last night I started all over again. I went through everyone I could think of, but all my contacts came up short."

"What about that other foundation grant you applied for last year? Did you apply again?"

"Yeah, but that never comes through," Natalia

answered. "I don't even know why I still apply. Getting monies for the Teen Dream Center is a long shot when it comes to that grant. It's past fantasyland and into the realm of 'Ain't never gonna happen in this lifetime.'"

"Don't say that," Nikita sympathized. "Anything's possible."

"You know I'm a realist, so believe me when I say not this."

"But you still applied?" Nikita asked.

Natalia nodded and sighed heavily. "The last thing I want to do is tell the kids that I failed and it's over."

"Trust me, I know that won't happen." Nikita reached over and gently touched her older sister's arm. "Nat, I have money saved. Take it and do what you need to do. If you need more, you know Dominik, Mikhail, Tatiana and Stephen want to help, not to mention the rest of the family."

"No, I can't take your money, Niki, or theirs. That's not how it works. It's a nonprofit organization, not a family thing. It's all about funding through grants. If I want Teen Dream to thrive and grow, I need to do this the right way." She sat back and looked around. A man seated right next to their table immediately caught her eye. It wasn't what he was doing that piqued her interest, it was what he wasn't doing. He was dressed inconspicuously. He kept his head bowed low into a newspaper, yet there was something about him that seemed odd, at least to her.

"Nat, don't worry. Everything will work out."

"I don't see how," she said, shifting her attention back to her sister. "It just makes me so mad. They profess to want to help kids. Then they sit up there on their high perches and with just a few signatures destroy children's lives. They gave no reasons other than that the grant money would be better served elsewhere. Are you kidding me? What does that even mean?"

"Everything will work out, just as it's supposed to. I have a good feeling about this and you know I know these things."

Natalia smiled and nodded, but she still wasn't reassured by her sister's comforting words. Although she was right about one thing: Nikita had a way of knowing when things were going to work out. She had definite instincts and ever since childhood she'd learned to trust those instincts. Since then they had led her to an enviable culinary career all around the world and now back here to Key West.

"Here, taste. You'll feel much better after just one bite," Nikita offered from the small tray of treats she'd placed in front of them when she sat down.

"Niki, your sensual delights, as amazingly sinful as they are, won't fix this. I'm running out of time and out of money even faster. I figure I only have until mid-May to find a sponsor for the center. I'm giving myself until Mother's Day. Seems appropriate."

"Do you think that…" Nikita began.

"I don't want to go there." Natalia held her hand up, interrupting quickly, knowing exactly what her sister was thinking.

"You're thinking the same thing, aren't you? Clay Sullivan did it. He blackballed you just as he threatened," Nikita said.

"I don't want to go there," Natalia repeated.

"Why not?" Nikita continued. "It's a very real

possibility and it needs to be addressed. Let's face it: the jerk is a pathetic excuse for a man. And he calls himself a philanthropist. Please, he's more like a horny, Viagra-soaked con man."

"And thankfully I found out in time to get out before contracts were signed."

"He's a jerk and a womanizer and a thug who deserves to have his checkbook cut off," Niki added. Natalia chuckled at her sister's clever phrasing. "And if he thinks that I haven't spread the word to every woman within earshot, then he's mistaken."

"Can we please change the subject now?" Natalia asked.

"Fine, but you know I'm right. He did it."

"Subject change, please," Natalia repeated.

"Fine, fine. So are you ready to be left alone this weekend?"

"I'll miss my guys, but after the morning I'm having, most definitely," Natalia said. "It's been one insane disaster after another. You wouldn't believe the craziness and it's not even noon yet."

"One of those, huh?" Nikita asked. Natalia nodded woefully. "So, what are your plans for this weekend?"

"You know, the usual. Meet a gorgeous man, fly off to an exotic island and have dinner on the beach. Or paint the kitchen and trim the trees in the front yard."

"I like the first one better," Nikita said.

"Me, too, but we both know that's not gonna happen. So back to the real world. I'm going to get some work done, paint the kitchen Saturday morning and then do some gardening the rest of the weekend."

"Working, painting and gardening—come on, Nat,

you haven't had a day off since Brice was born. That's almost three years ago." Natalia noticed that the man at the next table looked up instantly. Earlier he hadn't moved an inch, but something got his attention now. Again his presence bothered her. This time she knew why. She recognized him; at least she thought she did.

Their eyes met, and in that one instant, even through his thick reading glasses, heavy brows, rough graying beard and lowered cap, she made out who she thought was David Montgomery. He was heavier, thicker around the middle, and the nose was all wrong. However, why would David Montgomery be in Key West?

The actor she'd seen onscreen was muscular, athletic and most definitely mouthwateringly gorgeous. The man at the table smiled halfheartedly. She nodded pleasantly then turned her attention back to her sister's comments.

"…so in my opinion you need to do something really exciting. I have an idea. Forget about painting. I'll get somebody to work for me and we'll go to Miami or Fort Lauderdale for a spa weekend special—just the two of us."

"Umm, a day at the spa really does sound tempting, but…"

"No buts, no second guesses. Come on now, don't wimp out on me," her sister warned. "You're a woman, not just a social worker and a mom. You need to do something for yourself sometimes. You know the boys will be fine. You told me that Stephen and Mia bought out half the toy store when they volunteered to babysit this weekend. You know they're really looking forward to this and you definitely need some time off."

"All right, let's do it. But how about going for just one day to the day spa at the Keys Gateway Hotel?"

"Sounds perfect," Nikita agreed.

"I'll make the reservations for Sunday, but right now I need to get back to the office. I have a million things to take care of before I pick up the boys this evening. I'll call you and let you know the appointment time." She took one last glance at the man intent on being inconspicuous. His head was buried in the newspaper and his cap had been lowered even more. David Montgomery was a ridiculous notion. She was upset and it was obviously just her imagination.

David had always been a student of human nature. He'd watched and learned as numerous scenes just like the previous one unfolded in cafés and diners all over the country. This was his studio. Some actors went to classes, learning techniques mastered by countless thespians before them. David didn't; he sought out the real thing. It was one thing to practice emotion. It was definitely another to see it actually revealed.

As an actor, his job was to mimic reality and that, coupled with an added dimension, brought that reality to the screen. Countless awards, a staggering number of accolades and pronounced notoriety proved that he did his job very well. But this time he wasn't on an undercover research trip. This was his life. This was to save his career and everything else he knew.

He had glanced at the women at the table next to him unnoticed a few times. They were attractive and most definitely favored each other. Both had soft facial features with full lips and high cheeks. Their eyes were dark, framed by thick long lashes. One had short hair with lighter highlights and wore jeans and a white T-shirt with the bakery's name printed on the front. The other, dressed more conservatively in a slim, knee-length skirt and sleeveless blouse wrapped in front, with hair pulled up in a relaxed bun, was slightly curvier and more feminine. She was the one who had noticed him.

As an observer, being noticed was always a risk. But lately he'd narrowed that danger down vastly by varying techniques. Disguises and props were a must, of course. He carried a supply of glasses, beards, mustaches and wigs to change his appearance. He also had padded clothing and an array of rubber and gelatin prosthetic devices that he could affix to his face and body. They changed his appearance, helping him to blend in as seamlessly as possible. But it seemed as if this time it didn't work. One of the women was looking at him suspiciously. She seemed to recognize him even though he had no idea how or why. She didn't say anything, so he assumed he'd succeeded.

Moments later he watched as the two women stood and hugged. Then one woman walked out the front door and the other walked behind the counter and entered the kitchen. He also noticed that the woman at the next table was looking at him strangely. He quickly gathered the rest of his meal into the take-out bag and tossed it in the trash can on his way out the door.

As soon as he got outside, he called his assistant, Pamela. "Hey, I've been waiting for you to call," she began. "Where are you now?"

"I'm back in Key West."

"Finally. David, seriously, you need to get some rest. You can't keep flying all over the place, plus trying to figure all this out. You're gonna burn out."

"I'm fine. I found her. At least I think I did. She's one of the two women we discussed, Natalia Coles."

"Are you absolutely positive?"

"Not entirely."

"Well, I tried to get birth records from the local hospital, but they're permanently sealed for family privacy. I couldn't even get into the computer, so their system must be airtight. I'm at the local newspaper office, going through old files, looking for birth announcements to compare dates. Apparently, they don't list them online."

"That's one good thing, I suppose. If you can't get to the hospital birth records or birth announcements, no one else can, either."

"Exactly."

"We have to work fast," David insisted. "I can't wait for the attorneys. So I'm going to need more information."

"Hold on, I just found two birth announcements. You were right, it's Natalia Coles. Her second child was three weeks premature."

"Two announcements. That means two kids," he said slowly.

"Yes," Pamela confirmed.

Exasperated, he sighed heavily. "I need to see this. Send me a copy of the newspaper announcements." He disconnected and a few seconds later his phone beeped, indicating that he'd just received an embedded e-mail. He opened it, saw the photo of her and read the announcement. He called his assistant again. "I need to know what I can expect and exactly how big of a threat this woman is going to be. That means I need to know who she is—everything, from her elementary school to what she's doing next week. You got that?"

"Yeah, I got it. But David, why don't you just let your attorneys handle this now? That's why you pay them."

"I need to end this personally. I want answers. For that I'll have to confront her and probably pay her off."

"Are you kidding?" Pamela said, stunned. "You can't just walk up to a complete stranger and say, 'Hey, I'm the biological father of your two children. Here's some money to keep your mouth shut.'"

"Believe me, everybody has a price. She did this for a reason. I intend to find out what that reason is and end this once and for all."

"She probably doesn't even know about you. The clinic said that everything was confidential."

"If that's the case, then I'll find that out, as well. But the end result is that I'm going to put this to rest. What else is going on?"

"Okay," she said skeptically. "Your favorite reporter, Beck, has been calling me all morning. He called me three times since last night. He wants an interview."

David groaned. Beck was a tabloid and blog reporter who had covered him ever since his career began. Then, when his career skyrocketed, Beck became insatiable. He was like David's own personal bloodhound, constantly following him and searching for dirt. His focus was exclusively on David, and it seemed that ferreting out any hint of wrongdoing committed by him was his calling. The last thing David needed was to have a dogged entertainment reporter on his back. "Stall him, put him off. Tell him I'm incapacitated. I'll call him in a few weeks."

"I tried that already and you know he doesn't work like that. He knows you've flown all over, plus he's in one of his determined moods. He wants to know why you're down here in Key West when technically you're supposed to be on set."

David groaned again. "Tell him the truth. The movie's been pushed back for two months. He can pick up the details in the trades. Instead of hanging out in L.A. or traveling, I'm chillin' here and I'm scouting locations for a personal project. No big deal."

"Okay, but you know how he is when he gets a lead. It's like he can smell drama about to happen. He said that he's headed down in this direction at the end of the week. He wants to set up an interview when he gets here."

"Where is he now?"

"I don't know, but I can find out," she said.

"Find out, be discreet, then tell him I'll be in the same area and I'll give him an interview there."

"Do you really think he suspects?" she asked.

"I don't know. Maybe. I do know that I don't need this right now." He thought for a moment. "Tell the attorneys to just file the papers. It's time to end this."

"Are you sure? You don't even know the whole story yet."

He had planned to remain impersonal, but the fact was, this was a very personal matter and the reality of his predicament was beginning to sink in. "Yeah, I'm positive. Do it."

"Okay, but that might be a problem at the moment. The clinic's attorneys are involved now."

"Meaning?" he asked.

"Meaning that since the lab prematurely sold your sample, the clinic is cooperating up to a point. They still insist on protecting their client by invoking the privileged information rule. It will go into the hands of a judge soon."

"This is ridiculous. There's a woman walking around here with a loaded uterus pointed at my career and I'm just supposed to sit waiting, doing nothing and running out of time. This is a nightmare."

"David, they're doing everything they can at this point."

"It's not good enough," he said hotly. "Meet me back at the suite. Oh, one last thing: find out what kind of money problems she's having. She mentioned a center. Find out what it is."

"Got it. I'll see you later."

"Right. I'm on my way to the docks to change. Then I intend to meet this woman."

David closed his cell and looked down the street in the direction he had watched her walk. The streets were crowded with tourists and residents, yet no one recognized him. He walked slowly, purposefully, shoulders hunched and head down. Each step he took fueled his anger more and more. The same fire that was burning in her eyes earlier burned just as intensely in his gut right now.

She was clearly angry, about what he didn't care. All he cared about was that she kept her mouth shut. If it took money, he'd pay, no matter what the cost.

He opened his cell and looked down at the newspaper photo again. The fire in her eyes was missing. She was happy. But the threat she posed to his life was still very real. She was the mother of his children and one way or the other he was going to make sure she and her children were permanently out of his life.

Chapter 2

The day that had started out trying turned dismal as the hours progressed. By four o'clock that afternoon, Natalia sat at her desk assessing her options and reviewing strategies as she gathered together paperwork from the frustrating child custody court case that she'd been working on for weeks. It had been postponed twice, leaving her fifteen-year-old charge in foster care limbo each time. This time she was able to petition the court to award the paternal grandmother temporary custody.

In another case, a teenager had run away and then was picked up for shoplifting. She was sent to the teen detention center. Natalia arranged for full family visitation and a family law attorney to take the case pro bono. Fortunately, from her last conversation with the parents and attorney, everything was on track to turn out fine.

And to top it all off, she'd been having a daylong

debate with the manager of a rental property since nine that morning. He'd served eviction papers on a family of six. The manager was an obstinate jerk, lacking the least bit of human compassion. He completely refused to extend the family credit, asserting that they were a risk he was uncomfortable taking. Since the father had just gotten a new job, she'd hoped that would change his mind. It hadn't. Jerk. She was now reviewing the paperwork, searching for some kind of loophole to reverse his decision. So far she had come up empty.

Letting young people down because the system had failed them was the worst thing she could imagine. She immediately thought about the teen center and the funding that had fallen through. Keeping it open would mean a place for at-risk teens to hang out when they had nowhere else to go. The alternative was the streets. She needed to find a way to keep the doors open, even though she had less than two months to do it. She was determined to find a solution; as usual she stayed focused.

The knock on her door didn't distract her. This late in the afternoon, a knock could only mean one thing: the courthouse was finally sending over the foster care paperwork she'd been expecting all day. They were always running behind and she was always bailing them out, but sending the courthouse clerk and Natalia's friend, Helen Parker, always eased the rush. Sitting at her desk, she didn't even bother looking up from the laptop's monitor to see who was at her door.

"Hey, Helen, you're late, as usual. I know you need everything ASAP. Do me a favor and drop the file on the chair with my briefcase by the door." She casually pointed across the room. "I'll read it tonight and have it delivered to the courthouse Monday morning. Thanks, and have a good night."

"Uhh, Ms. Coles, Mom wanted me to give this to you personally."

Hearing a pubescent squeak instead of Helen's cheerful chatter, Natalia stopped reading and looked up. Helen's oldest son stood awkwardly at the door, dressed in his soccer uniform and holding a manila envelope.

"Hi, Jake," Natalia said, standing and greeting him. "On your way to a soccer game?"

He nodded. "My mom's waiting outside in the car. She said that since I can run faster than she can I should bring this to you. We're late."

Natalia chuckled. "Okay, set it on the chair. Thanks, Jake. Tell your mom I'll call her Monday." He did as instructed.

"Okay, I will. Bye, Ms. Coles." He turned and ran.

"Have a good game, and be careful," she called after him a few seconds before she heard the front door close soundly. Sitting down again, she took a moment to think about what her two boys would be like when they got older. Then she thought about what they'd look like. At birth and for the first year or so it was obvious that they both resembled their biological father. Their light eyes were definitely not from her. But as soon as Brice turned two, his looks began to change and become more defined. His eyes, once light, had darkened to a softer light brown with golden flecks, and his button nose and warm smile were definitely hers. Now, at nearly three years old, his looks were changing again.

Natalia sat at her desk as a stray thought passed

through her mind. It was the same one she'd been considering lately. It was about the father of her boys. Everything from the very beginning had been clinical, rational and precise. She'd gone to one of the foremost in vitro fertilization specialists in the country and after a myriad of diagnostic tests she'd chosen the sample with the best attributes. Statistically, her children would be exceptional. It might have seemed cold and calculating to some, but she was determined to give her children the best.

Specimen number 0082911087 was African American, genetically healthy, with an above average IQ. He was noted as tall, athletic and having exceptional physical attributes. She'd purchased the sample and then been artificially inseminated by the same donor twice. Hence her sons had the same mother and father, but the curious question still haunted her. What was the father really like? The doctor, the clinic, the procedure were all top rate. She'd chosen a clinic in L.A. because it was the best in the country with a success rate that was unparalleled. Still, there were no guarantees.

Brushing the random thoughts aside, she went back to her current crisis. She began going through old records, current data and retro cases involving family rent disputes. Not finding much, she went online to several sites that were usually helpful. They were, showing amicable resolutions in most cases. Satisfied that she'd found a glimmer of hope for the rental problem, Natalia exited the Web sites and then saw a photo of David Montgomery on her refreshed host home page.

He'd just been named to the "Sexiest Man Alive" list. She immediately thought about the foundation grant she had applied for. So far she hadn't received a rejection letter, but that didn't mean anything. The Montgomery Foundation had been set up by actor-philanthropist David Montgomery, and it distributed grants to programs dedicated to helping at-risk teens and youths.

She opened the screen and read through the main premise of the foundation again. Of all the celebrity-sponsored organizations and foundations, his was by far the most generous and the one most suited for what she wanted to achieve with the Teen Dream Center.

She looked over the sites-listed screens for the hundredth time. Scrolling through the foundation's requirements, she noted the Montgomery Foundation Grant award date was still a few days away. When applying, she'd been meticulous in preparing the proposal and she knew that the last part of the proposal application process was an on-site interview. She took a deep, hopeful breath. Getting a call for a personal interview would be a godsend. Getting an award letter would be a saving grace. There was a minuscule chance; still, the possibility definitely made her smile. She quickly went back and read the main article on David Montgomery.

Curious, she drifted to other sites dedicated to David Montgomery. There were hundreds—no, thousands—most fan-based and some official. Others were created by obviously love-struck fans enamored of his big-screen image. She was amazed at the ridiculous things they did to get his attention, some more preposterous than others.

She continued scanning the stream of articles, stopping

periodically to read something of interest. She opened a file that listed his professional accomplishments. His listing of movies was impressive, even more so than she originally thought. The next site she entered was the official David Montgomery Web site. Instantly his smiling face and ever-popular dimpled grin flashed on the screen. She read quotes and watched a few streaming podcast interviews. She obviously didn't know him, but by all accounts he appeared more like a mysterious accidental superstar. His movies grossed millions and he'd been dubbed the sexiest man alive by several magazines. *Sexiest Star, Beautiful Person* and *Most Powerful in Hollywood* were just a few honors bestowed on him.

In public, he appeared unfazed by the media attention. He didn't appear to be arrogant or full of himself, as she assumed most celebrities were. He actually seemed to be a nice guy on and off the screen. But she knew that could all be fake, as well. After all, nothing in Hollywood was real.

She flipped through picture after picture, seeing his smiling face and a parade of women at his side. David Montgomery was gorgeous, rich and talented—women seemed drawn to him like magnets.

Eventually, she glanced at the open file sitting on her desk and went back to work. After ten minutes she'd come up with several ideas to help the family stay in the rental, but none of them seemed guaranteed. She laid her head down on her desk just for a moment to still her thoughts. The stress of everything was getting to her. A weekend break was exactly what she needed, but she knew that as long as she stayed in the area she'd be working. A few minutes later, there was another knock on the door. "Did you forget something, or is the game over already?" she joked.

"Neither."

The deep masculine voice was totally wrong. Natalia looked up quickly. A second later she glanced at her computer monitor and then back up at the man in the doorway. There was no mistake. It was David Montgomery, movie star, standing there: rugged, powerful, successful and handsome as all get out. The man was even better looking in person—if that was possible.

David Montgomery wore dark sunglasses, a baseball cap and a fitted polo shirt that accentuated his narrow waist, well-defined chest and broad shoulders. The headline Sexiest Man Alive glared out at her from the corner of her eye. *Good Lord, he's perfection. The man is flawless.* Even in the dark sunglasses and lowered cap he was utterly gorgeous, and the thoughts that were zipping through her mind were purely sinful.

Her eyes shifted down his body. His long muscular legs were bowed just enough to give him that cool swagger that made women swoon. He wore jeans on what she knew was a magnificent body, since she had seen him naked on film. *Omigod, that's right. I've seen him naked.* Well, she and about a hundred million others had seen him naked and from the back. The mental flash of one film's scene showing him in the shower with his muscular cheeks took her by surprise. She bit her lower lip and stood up slowly, trying to get a grip and erase that particular scene from her thoughts. It didn't work. "Hi, hello," she finally managed to say.

"Natalia Coles?" he asked. She nodded then watched as he strolled in and stood in front of her desk. "We need to talk."

She smiled and nodded again as her heartbeat's rhythm went into overdrive and every nerve in her body sizzled. This was it, the personal interview that meant her program was one step closer to getting the foundation grant and staying alive. She noted that he didn't smile. He just stood there, stoic and staring, completely expressionless. He was definitely different from the seemingly friendly, good-natured guy he portrayed so well on- and offscreen. But of course, this was business and she intended to ask him for a lot of money, so professional it was. "Yes, we do. Thank you so much for coming."

"My name is…" he began.

"I know who you are," she interrupted, of course seeing through the ridiculous disguise. He removed his cap and dark glasses. Tired, gray eyes stared back at her. "Much better," she said.

"You obviously recognized me." He walked farther into the office. His rugged swagger seemed even more pronounced than on the big screen.

"I suppose there's a tribe on the outskirts of New Guinea who might not know who you are. Possibly, but I doubt it. Yes, I recognized you, Mr. Montgomery. Thank you for coming." She extended her hand to shake. He reciprocated. They each held on an instant longer than necessary. "I apologize. I'm a bit flushed and unprepared at the moment. I didn't expect you to come here. I assumed you wanted to meet at the…"

"So you were expecting me to come," he said, interrupting her.

"I hoped, but actually, I didn't expect you to come in person. I presumed you had a staff or attorneys who handled things like this."

"And you know why I'm here," he said.

"Yes, of course. As I mentioned, I don't have the complete package here with me at the moment. Perhaps we can set up a meeting tomorrow afternoon at the center. I'll be happy to show you around and have you meet the kids. I know they'll be delighted to meet you. I can also arrange for *The Citizen,* our local newspaper, to come out and…"

"Absolutely not. We do this now and get it over with." He sat down. "Since this is obviously a very delicate matter, I'd like to keep this between us and our attorneys. No publicity."

"Sure, if you'd prefer," she said, puzzled by his comment. "But I assumed your publicists would be sending out press releases or something of that nature. Publicity like this would certainly be a tremendous benefit for the kids."

He stiffened as he realized her veiled threat of exposure. The last thing he intended to do was make this public. "No press, no publicity. There will be a nondisclosure agreement forwarded to you. The only reason I'm here now is that I wanted to meet the woman who could do something like this."

She nodded. "So I presume you have a few questions for me regarding the proposal I sent you."

"Your proposal?" he queried, slightly confused.

"Yes, I can print out a copy if you'd like. As a matter

of fact, I was just going through a few details to clarify my position and give you a better idea about what I had in mind."

David eyed her curiously. He wasn't sure what game she was playing, but whatever it was, he didn't intend to lose. "Yes, do that. I definitely want to know what you have in mind."

He watched as she turned to her computer and began typing. An instant later, he heard the printer begin to work. She stood and walked to the credenza behind her desk. He took the opportunity to assess her more thoroughly. She seemed so matter-of-fact about everything. She certainly wasn't what he expected. But then again, he had no idea what to expect.

She was attractive—there was no doubt about that. Her brown skin looked soft and touchable. She had full, kissable lips; soft, soulful, dark-as-sin eyes; perky, rounded breasts; a slender waist. And when she turned around, a tight, apple-shaped rear that instantly and unexpectedly set his body on fire. She wore a gray, fitted skirt and a matching low-cut blouse with a thick black leather belt and black high heels. His body lurched and his mouth went dry just looking at her. But he wasn't here for that. He took one last glance at her long wraparound legs and then looked away. She was affecting him in ways he hadn't expected, and his body was reacting. He closed his eyes and lowered his head to refocus. This woman could destroy his career and everything he cared about. The only thing he needed to do now was focus on that.

"Excuse me for saying this, but you don't look so

good. Are you all right? Is everything okay?" she asked, seeing his eyes closed and his head down.

"I wanted to talk to you before the attorneys get involved," he began.

She nodded. "Sure, okay."

"I have a few questions for you." She nodded again, indicating that he should continue. "First, how did you know that it was my—" He paused to rephrase the question. "Why did you choose me for this?"

"Actually, I did check out a number of other options, but truthfully, I like what you seem to represent in your career and personal life. Your foundation is extraordinary. But it's not all about the money, although we certainly need that. You seem to have a core honesty and decency that I think will be a huge, positive influence on the children, and if you'd like to take a more personal interest in them, that can most certainly be arranged."

"How much do you know about me—my family history?"

She grimaced. These questions didn't seem to pertain to the grant application, but she answered. "Only what I've read."

"And how much do you want from me?" he asked.

"Whatever you're willing to give. Everything is outlined in this proposal." She walked around her desk and handed him the folder. "Your ongoing contributions will ensure that our kids will have the very best money can buy. When I send the progress reports I'm sure you'll…"

"Hold it right there." He took the proposal, stood and tossed it on her desk without even bothering to glance at it. "Ongoing contributions? Progress reports?" he asked quickly.

"Yes." She turned as her proposal slid across her desk and then stopped beside her keyboard.

"No. One payment—that's all you're gonna get from me," he said.

"But the kids are going to need ongoing support. I was under the impression that it was an ongoing…"

"Enough." He knew that he had taken her by surprise. She opened her mouth to answer, but nothing came out. "No more proposals, no more dancing around the issue. I know you have an amount in mind. What is it? What do you want?"

She walked back behind her desk, shaking her head. "I'm sorry. This isn't how I expected this interview to go. Perhaps we should postpone this until our attorneys can…"

"No. No postponements. We finish this now," he cut her off quickly. "Just give me your price so we can end this. I want nothing more to do with it, understood? Also, I want everything that's left."

She was completely confused. "I don't understand. Left from what?"

"Don't play games with me. I have no intention of doing this drama with you every two years or whenever you feel the need. This is a one-time deal, under the table, no records, no paperwork. Now how much do you want?"

"Actually, this is a legal transaction. It doesn't work like that," she said, becoming annoyed. "I can't just give you a number and…"

"Look," he interrupted briskly, "if you want to play

this game with me, I assure you I will win and you'll get nothing. I don't have to do this. There's no legal obligation binding me to you or your kids. If you want to take it to court, that's fine, too. Just make sure that's what you want."

"Are you overmedicated, rude or just nuts?" Natalia asked, moving quickly to turn off her computer. "You keep talking about games… Do you mind elaborating on that for those of us in the cheap seats who don't have a clue as to what you're talking about?"

"You know exactly what I'm talking about."

Her cell phone rang. She glanced down at the caller ID number. It was the nursery school. "Excuse me, I need to get this."

The phone conversation was brief and as far as she was concerned had instantly ended their interview. "I need to go now." She grabbed her purse and suit jacket. "This is the proposal." She picked it up and handed it to him again. "I'll be more than happy to discuss it with you at your convenience, but right now I need to go."

"What happened?" he asked, knowing that the phone call had changed something. Her expression had changed. She was troubled and her voice broke and trembled.

"I have to go," she repeated.

"Go where?" he asked quickly.

She looked at him curiously. "I have to get to the nursery school."

"Nursery school?"

"Yes, my son had an accident."

David's heart suddenly lurched. He never expected to feel anything when it came to his sired children, so the instant concern was surprising. "Let me drive. You're upset."

She looked at him questioningly. "That's okay. I'm fine." She quickly crossed the office and grabbed her briefcase and the envelope Jake had left on the chair. He followed and stood watching her as she opened the case and stuffed the envelope inside.

"Is there anything I can do to help?" he asked. She looked at him and shook her head. "Look, I'm trying to do the right thing here. I don't want to seem indelicate, but none of this is my doing, nor is it my responsibility. I'm only here because of future implications."

She turned to him. "You are an exceptional actor, because you pull off that nice guy personality flawlessly. But right now, I have someplace else to be. Here's my card. Perhaps we can have a more coherent conversation another time. It was—interesting meeting you."

David looked down at the business card she handed him, then back up just in time to see the sweet sway of her hips as she hurried down the hall. The sexy sight caught him off guard, sending an instant rush of hot blood sizzling through his body, ending in his hardened discomfort. He pulled out his cell and called his assistant. Pamela answered on the first ring.

"How'd it go?" she asked.

"Good question. She was evasive and pretended that she had no idea what was going on. She kept talking about a proposal." He glanced at the folder in his hand. "Either she has no idea about my relationship to her sons or she's a better actor then I am."

"That might make sense," Pamela said.

"What do you mean?" he asked.

"I got some information on Natalia Coles. Her Web site says that she's a family psychologist with the police, plus she also founded a local center for at-risk teens called the Teen Dream Center. It's become very popular and she's been getting some really good press lately. I also found out that it's publicly funded by donations, endowments and grants."

"Grants from organizations such as the Montgomery Foundation?" he asked.

"Yes. She's applied for the grant the past three years, but didn't get it. Chances are she probably thinks you're here about that."

David nodded. "That would explain a lot."

"It also looks like maybe she bought your sperm without knowing who you are. Of course, all she knew were your vital statistics and a number. It makes sense. The clinic didn't know who you were until you told them."

"Do me a favor. Get me more information on this teen center. I want to know everything about it for the next time we talk."

"Next time?" she asked, surprised.

"What? You didn't think this was over, did you? Check me into the hotel. It's time to go to work," he said as he walked down the hall to the exit. He stepped outside just as she drove away.

"I thought you just wanted to know if she was some kind of con woman and a threat to your career."

"I'm not a hundred percent satisfied yet. I want to know more about her—about them."

"So want are you going to do—just start asking

questions about her and her kids? I don't think that'll work."

"No, I have something more creative in mind."

This was crazy. Natalia glanced back in the rearview mirror and saw David Montgomery walking out of the building. She had no idea what had just happened. Maybe he was testing her. Maybe he was just nuts. Either way, she couldn't deal with it right now. She turned her attention back to getting to her son.

Even though the nursery school director had assured her that Brice was just fine, she knew that she'd feel better being with him. Ten minutes later, she looked down at the clock on her dashboard as she pulled into the nursery school parking lot. There were other parents picking up children. She waved as she hurriedly proceeded inside. As soon as she walked in she saw her sons. Her face, her smile and her day instantly brightened.

Family was everything to Natalia. That's why she'd chosen to enrich her life with two adorable children. Having a man in her life at this point wasn't nearly as important. It wasn't because she'd had her heart broken once too often, although that was certainly the truth. It wasn't because she was waiting around for Mr. Right to come and sweep her off her feet. Ultimately, her Mr. Right had turned out to be an anonymous donor, and it had been the perfect solution.

Seeing her boys made everything all right. Their smiling faces erased the previous half hour instantly. Brice was, as usual, building with his blocks. He built them high, then laughed hysterically when they fell down. Jayden sat nearby and, taking his cue from Brice, he laughed, rocked and bounced each time the blocks tumbled, as well.

Natalia smiled so hard she nearly burst into tears. This is why she did what she did and this was the joy she wanted all mothers to know, the feeling that their children were safe and happy and most of all loved.

She thought about her conversation with David Montgomery. It was strange, awkward and disjointed. So what if he was nuts or overmedicated? His foundation was by far the most promising and could benefit her center in numerous ways. He had all the programs already in place; she could very easily incorporate her dreams and ideas into his plan. All she had to do was make it work.

Natalia picked up her sons and stopped to see her brother at the hospital. She looked forward to the rest of the evening devoid of high drama and one crisis after the other. She was happy to go back to her simple, ordinary life, knowing that tomorrow was another day. And tomorrow she'd have to find a way to connect with David Montgomery again. She needed him—that much was certain. Getting him was the problem, but that was tomorrow's problem.

Chapter 3

"So how's Brice?" Nikita asked as she and Natalia placed their teacups on the table in front of the bakery and sat down. It was their usual morning routine. Nikita would take a short break from working in the bakery since dawn and Natalia would stop by after dropping her sons off and before heading to the office.

"He's fine. He was banging his building blocks together and hit himself in the head. The nursery school policy is to notify the parent of any accident, and since he also drew blood and required antiseptic and a Band-Aid, they asked me to pick him up early. When they called and I heard him crying in the background, my heart sank. I couldn't get there fast enough. After picking him up, I stopped by the hospital before going home. Dominik took a look at him, just to be on the safe side."

"It's nice having a big brother who's also a doctor."

"Tell me about it. After a very serious discussion on block building safety and a green lollipop, Brice was as good as new."

"I don't know how you do it sometimes. You work all day as a family psychologist with the police, you put in a full day's work at the center in the evenings and on top of all that you're a mom to two incredible boys. Motherhood is hard enough and being a single mother is just crazy."

"No, not crazy, challenging. But so very worth it," Natalia said, smiling. Nikita nodded in complete agreement. "That's why I want the center to succeed so badly. If I can make this happen, there'll be so many teens and families who will benefit from it."

"Hey, you're preaching to the choir. I'm a hundred percent behind you on this. You know that."

She smiled in gratitude. "I know. And thanks so much for all your support. I just wish I could get David Montgomery's foundation on board. He's my last hope."

"Speaking of David Montgomery," Nikita began, "I don't suppose you've seen this morning's entertainment section of the *Citizen?*"

"No, why?"

Nikita grabbed a newspaper from the next table and peeled out the entertainment section to show her. She turned to the page and handed it to her sister. "He's here, and it appears that his boat has been docked at our brother's place for the past week and a half. Someone took a photo of him leaving there yesterday."

Natalia shook her head. "I just spoke with Mikhail a few days ago. He didn't mention anything about this.

Looks like I'm going to have to have a nice long talk with our dear brother about his loyalties. He should have told me. He knew I applied for that grant."

"You know he wouldn't do that. Chances are he gave his word and you know how he can be when it comes to trust issues."

"Still," Natalia said, then shook her head, "it probably doesn't matter anyway after yesterday. I don't know how we left it."

"Whoa, back up. Left what with who?" Nikita exclaimed. "Exactly what happened yesterday?"

"That's right. With all the excitement with Brice and his cut I didn't get a chance to tell you that David Montgomery stopped by my office yesterday afternoon. I looked up and he was just standing there in my doorway."

"David Montgomery stopped by your office yesterday and you didn't think to tell me until now?" Nikita asked rhetorically.

Natalia nodded. "He just strolled right in and stood there."

"Now you're just bragging," Nikita said.

"Hardly. The personal interview is the last part of the grant application process. Actually, I've never even gotten that far in the past. After everything that happened yesterday with the letters about the city and state grants, I was thrilled that I was at least still in the running for his foundation's grant. But then the whole interview turned odd. It was like he had no idea about the grant application I had sent in or the center. It was just strange."

"What do you mean strange?" she asked, puzzled.

"He was asking me how much money I wanted. The thing is, it's a grant. The amount is set and distributed four times a year."

"Maybe he was just confused," Nikita offered, hoping to add clarity to a muddled situation. "Men like him have a million things on their minds."

"Maybe. I don't know." She shrugged, considering her sister's comment.

"Well, I hope you're happy. You're stealing the perfect man away from millions of women."

"Believe me, I'm not stealing anyone and they can have him, as far as I'm concerned. You know, I always heard that movie-star types were either mental cases or on the verge of becoming seriously deranged."

"Is that your professional, objective opinion?"

"The man's a nutcase. That's my professional opinion. I can only hope he has sensible people working on his foundation staff. It would be just my luck that he has the Mad Hatter as the appointed chairman."

"You've just ruined my fantasy."

"You? What about me?" she complained. "I've seen his television series and just about every one of his movies. His eyes are what fantasies are made of and his body—Lord, don't even get me started. When he stood there yesterday in the flesh, I thought I was dreaming. He is seriously gorgeous." She sighed. "Portrait of a dreamer—that's me. I hate it when reality jumps up and head-butts you with the truth."

"At least your *perception* of the truth," Nikita corrected her sister as she commiserated about the details of the meeting she had had the day before. "Oh, come on. It couldn't have been that bad."

"It was worse than bad. It was a disaster. Another perfectly good fantasy shot down by reality. I may have to go back to square one and start looking for another foundation."

"Or maybe not," Nikita added, looking behind her sister and seeing a man she thought looked a lot like David Montgomery getting out of a car down the street and immediately being besieged by autograph seekers.

"Trust me…"

Nikita halted Natalia's complaint with her hand. "Nothing worth having ever comes easy—you know that. Like, remember when you decided you were ready to start a family? You did everything imaginable to prepare for it. It wasn't easy, but you did it and now you have two beautiful boys. So you had a problem yesterday. Since when have you ever walked away from a problem? You have a problem—handle it."

"Me, no, it wasn't me. It was him. The man's got an ego on steroids. I get it that he's a movie star and all, but helping those less fortunate is what he's supposed to be known for. All I know is that the man we've read about as being a humanitarian and a philanthropist and the man I met yesterday were two completely different guys."

"Maybe that's how he works. It's his foundation. Maybe they do things differently."

"Not that differently," Natalia said, looking across the street and waving at a neighbor. The outside café was perfectly located on the tree-lined main thoroughfare through town. It was surrounded by a designer boutique on one side and a bookstore on the other and had excellent foot traffic.

Nikita turned and waved, as well, then turned back to her sister and glanced over her shoulder. She was right. It *was* David Montgomery and he was coming right toward them. "I don't know, Natalia, something tells me this isn't over just yet. You can still turn this around."

"Probably, if I could meet with him again, but after yesterday, he's probably back on the West Coast or maybe in the Far East by now."

"Oh, I wouldn't be so sure about that if I were you," Nikita said with a knowing smile.

Nikita glanced over her sister's shoulder again, as David Montgomery was coming right toward them. He paused for a quick photo with a fan, but kept his eye on their table.

"I refuse to placate his pathetically delicate movie-star ego. Niki, when I said it didn't go well, that's an understatement. The man is arrogant and obviously believes his own hype and…"

"…and you're short-tempered and have tunnel vision when it comes to helping others and getting your center funded," Nikita continued for her.

"Fine, okay, I admit it," Natalia confessed reluctantly. "I guess my behavior wasn't completely professional, either. After all, I kind of suggested that he was an overmedicated, insane nutcase to his face. Maybe not exactly the best script for opening dialogue."

"Actually, you suggested that I was either over-medicated, rude or crazy. Good afternoon, ladies."

Nikita smiled as Natalia turned and looked up to

see David standing right beside their table. "Hi. David Montgomery," he said, beaming that famous smile at Nikita as he reached out to shake her hand. She took his hand and shook politely while still amused by her sister's stunned expression.

"Nice to meet you. I'm Nikita Coles, and I believe you've already met my sister Natalia."

"Yes, we have met. It's a pleasure to see you again, Ms. Coles. I hope your son is well. Nothing too serious?"

"He's good. Thanks for asking."

"May I join you, ladies?"

"Actually, Mr. Montgomery, I was just about to head inside," Nikita said. Natalia's expression instantly changed. She frowned at her sister, giving her the *Don't leave me* eye.

"Please, call me David," he said.

Nikita nodded. "David it is. I need to get back inside. I have a few cakes in the oven. So please take my seat."

"Mmm, I wondered what smelled so good. I presume that this is your place?" He turned, looking up at the brick-front bakery and awning. The sign above read Nikita's Place.

"Yes, it is."

"How's the food here?" he asked, directing the question to Nikita but looking at Natalia.

"Excellent," Niki responded.

"High praise," David said, glancing her way, then turning to smile at Natalia.

"It's well worth it," Natalia added.

"How about if I send you out a few samples and you can judge for yourself?" Nikita said.

"That sounds awesome, but unfortunately I can't stay long," he said, focusing his attention on Natalia again.

"I'll send out the samples. You can take them with you," Nikita said.

"Now that I'd appreciate," he said.

Just then a fan came up and asked for his autograph, and he graciously obliged, as two others bravely walked up to ask for candid photos.

While he was distracted, Nikita leaned toward her sister's ear, speaking quietly. "Is it me or is he having a hard time taking his eyes off you? The vibe is seriously there."

"You've been in the hot kitchen too long. The man's a mega movie star. He can get any woman he wants. I'm a social worker and the mother of two, not exactly the sexy, seductress type."

Nikita shook her head, knowing better. Nikita knew a thing or two about attraction and, pheromones aside, David Montgomery was definitely checking her sister out. "Okay, I'll be right back," Nikita said, then stood and winked at her sister before hurrying inside.

"May I?"

"Of course. Have a seat."

He sat down and smiled, waiting for her to speak first. He still wasn't satisfied that she was completely unaware of their connection. She was just about to speak when another young fan came up to the table and asked for an autograph. He signed the napkin and was asked to pose for a photo with him. David readily agreed and asked Natalia to take the picture. She did, and the young kid ran off proudly, holding tight to his new treasure.

"I'll bet that made his day," Natalia said without thinking.

"I hope it did. If it wasn't for him and others like him, I'd be out of a job."

"So you take this Hollywood thing very seriously."

"No, definitely not the Hollywood thing. I don't get swept up by the nonsense—that's all transitory. But I do take the responsibility of affecting other people's lives very seriously. I know that when I do even the simplest thing it can change a person's perception not only of me, but of the next actor and even the way they feel about themselves," he said with gravity, as if admonishing her for being superficial.

She nodded. "That's commendable. Few people seem to take responsibility for their actions these days."

"Do you?" he asked, already presuming to know the answer.

She looked into his eyes. They betrayed nothing, but there was something he wasn't saying. "Take responsibility, yes. I like to think I do." She paused then continued. "Is there something you'd like to tell me?"

"Like what?" he offered.

"That's why I'm asking. It seems to me that you have something on your mind, something other than the foundation grant I applied for. If you do, and it concerns me or the center, I'd like to know what it is." He relaxed back in the wicker chair and smiled without responding. A few seconds of wordless silence passed. "I believe the ball's back in your court."

He laughed, smiled and nodded. "You're a very interesting woman. I like that. You're going to be fun."

"What does that mean?" she asked.

"It means that I seldom meet people open enough to tell me exactly what they think. You're determined and very self-assured, and you seem to know exactly what you want."

"I wasn't fishing for compliments," she said.

"They weren't compliments. They were facts."

She looked at him, debating, and then she nodded once. "Thank you. You want to tell me the truth now?"

"Which truth?" he asked.

"The one that concerns me," she said.

"Later," he said simply.

"Now," she insisted.

He smiled again. "You are persistent, aren't you?"

"Oh, if you only knew," she said. Just then a fan came up and asked for an autograph. He obliged while she sat waiting. She had to admit that their exchange was entertaining. They were both apparently strong-willed. He turned back to her. "So where do we go from here?" she asked.

"I read over your proposal last night. Your center is very promising. You have some inspired and inspiring ideas."

"You sound surprised."

"Not at all. On the contrary, I'm extremely impressed." A waitress came out of the bakery with a clear take-out box filled with a variety of miniature pastries. She smiled deliriously, then placed a small shopping bag on the table and turned to leave. David called her back, thanked her and then gave her a very generous tip. "As I was saying, I'm impressed. I'd like to continue this conversation, but unfortunately I have a meeting. Could you stop by my hotel this evening so we can talk? I assure you my intentions are honorable and strictly professional."

She considered his offer a moment and then agreed. "Later this afternoon would be best for me. I already have plans this evening."

"A hot date?" he asked teasingly with a sly grin on his face.

"Yes, something like that," she said, smiling happily.

He continued grinning, but the tenseness pulling at his insides was troubling. Few could discern the convoluted range of emotions churning within him. He wasn't sure why her comment upset him so. It had never occurred to him that she was seeing someone. "Fine," he said tensely. "Keys Gateway Hotel. Four o'clock okay with you?"

She stood and nodded. "I'll see you at four."

David watched her leave, then he headed back to his hotel. It was still early and he wasn't in the mood to deal with his hordes of fans today. On the red carpet, at a movie premiere, on the set—sure, he'd do the Hollywood star thing. Even when he was out eating dinner, with a mouthful of tiramisu, he'd smile graciously and sign whatever piece of nonsense he'd been given. Most days he was cool with it; he even enjoyed it. Seeing admiring faces, accepting over-the-top accolades, being treated like royalty—hey, it was all part of the job. He always figured that he didn't get paid just to act; handling the promotion end of the business with finesse sent his income into the double-digit millions.

So it was all well and good being attacked by paparazzi and photo hounds, but when it was his personal time, he expected to fade into the background. High hopes indeed, since his soaring career had long since dictated otherwise. He was spotted everywhere he went, and it was close to a miracle that he'd lasted this long in the Key West area without being noticed. But he knew it wouldn't last. Late yesterday after he had cleaned up and changed his clothes at the docks, he noted that someone had taken a picture. Two hours later his publicist informed him that the photo was now circulating for purchase by local newspapers and the tabloids.

He tipped his cap lower, covered it with his hood, squared his shoulders and stalked briskly through the large hotel lobby. He avoided eye contact, knowing that people stared, wondering what a man dressed like a bum off the street was doing in the most expensive hotel in Key West. He expected security to stop him, but fortunately no one did, which was fine with him. He wasn't in the mood for drama.

He strolled to the elevator bank but kept going, finding the stairway, a much more private way up to his suite. Climbing fifteen flights of stairs wasn't much of a workout, but he needed the stress reducer. When he was working on set, he kept himself in peak condition. He had a personal trainer who tortured him daily, so to him this was merely a warm-up exercise.

He got to his floor, opened the stairway door and glanced down the hall in both directions. It was clear. He strode two doors down and knocked. The door opened almost instantly.

"Hey," Pamela said as she waved before returning her focus to her PDA and the heated phone conversation she was having. David brushed past her and walked into the suite. He headed to the open balcony doors as she closed the door to the suite and went back to the makeshift office area set up in the dining room.

He stepped out onto the balcony and looked around. From the top floor of the hotel, he could see the full, breathtaking brilliance of the Key West skyline. The expansive view was relatively flat and vibrantly colorful. The sky was crystal clear and the emerald-blue water of the Gulf of Mexico sparkled brilliantly in the distance. Any other time he would have loved to sit back, relax and enjoy the splendor of the city, but this wasn't a pleasure trip. This was business. He moved to the balcony rail and looked over, then down. Somewhere out there was a woman who could change his life forever. She had his children and the mere thought of it made him cringe.

It wasn't supposed to happen like this. When he'd made the one-time donation to the sperm bank ten years ago, he was a struggling actor. He was auditioning for the lead role in a new television action drama and needed to get to New York quickly. He was twenty-two, broke and desperate, and that one momentary lapse in judgment would probably ruin everything he had worked so hard to achieve. Ten years ago, he'd gotten the role. It was the start of everything for him—seven years on television and a movie career that had skyrocketed beyond belief. Now he needed to do serious damage control and get back what once belonged to him.

His nature was to be proactive, and not taking control made him feel stifled and useless. For the first time in a long time, his future was out of his hands. It was like being shuffled around from relative to relative when he was a child. He'd had no control then and he had none now. He hated it. He needed to do something. "Enough," he said, slamming his fist down on the rail.

"Morning," Pamela said as she pulled the Bluetooth from her ear and stepped out onto the balcony. "Your agent is about to get his credit cards canceled, have his business computer hijacked and his life turned upside down. You really need to reel him in before I do."

David sighed heavily. This wasn't what he needed to deal with today. "Morning," he replied, still staring out at Key West. "What's Lenny done now?"

"First of all, he acts like I work for him and I most certainly do not. I'm your personal assistant—not his. He actually has a list of things he wants me to do before we get back to L.A. Like I'm actually gonna do that."

"I'll talk to him," David said, reassuring her.

"Good. 'Cause one more of his comments about my creative investigations and he'll be looking at life in the Middle Ages up close and personal. That means no computer, no credit cards and no digital footprint at all."

David smiled, knowing that Pamela was very capable of backing up her threat. She was a genius when it came to computers. As a young teen, she and his sister, Brenda, got into trouble as a result of their computer creativity. They had broken into school records, department store customer accounts and even police files. Now, as an adult, she was just plain scary when it came to computers.

"Let me guess: dark sunglasses, baseball cap, hooded

jacket pulled up, insert laughter here. Of course, you know you're like Movie Star in Hiding 101," Pamela said as she walked farther out onto the balcony, seeing him still completely covered up in his disguise.

"Not in the mood today, Pam," he said dryly.

Hiring Brenda's best friend, Pamela Ray, was a stroke of brilliance, but sometimes he wondered if perhaps he'd drifted across the line into lunacy instead. Pamela was part Nancy Drew, part Wonder Woman, part Einstein and part pain in the neck. She was his personal assistant and had no illusions about their relationship, since the last thing he needed was an obsessed fan working for him. Her sole ambition was to have her own business of specialized assistants, a market completely untapped, given the reality of the business world.

Her job description was simple. Get whatever he needed, look out for whatever he missed, keep the unwanted attention away and keep him on schedule. She was brilliant at it.

"Seriously, is that outfit supposed to fool anybody?"

"For your information, it worked. No one even noticed me as I walked into the hotel lobby just now. They usually only notice me when I want them to."

Pamela shook her head. "Why is it that movie stars think all that disguise stuff is gonna work?" she asked. "That getup draws attention to you—not the other way around. Seriously, for a man who makes his living forever in makeup and costume, you should know that. Get rid of all that stuff and you'll just blend in with everyone else—trust me. Nobody will even notice you."

He coolly removed his dark sunglasses, dropped the hood and took off the cap. He turned and gave her the multimillion-dollar, heart-stopping, knee-weakening smile, dimple and all.

She shook her head. "You're right. Never mind."

Chapter 4

Instead of going back to her office, Natalia headed in the opposite direction. Twenty minutes later, she nodded to her brother's assistant and headed straight up to his office. This wasn't one of her usual, impromptu, end-of-the-day social visits where they'd sit around and joke. No, she was on a mission. He'd withheld important information from her and as far as she was concerned, he'd crossed the line. And whether he knew it or not, he was going to make this right. Furious, she gave him the murderous look.

"Hey, what's up?" Mikhail said, seeing his sister enter his office and cross to his desk. "I didn't know you were stopping by today." A second later he saw the fire in her eyes. He stood instantly. "What's wrong? What happened?"

She dropped the newspaper Nikita had given her on her brother's desk. He glanced down at the full-color photo of David Montgomery, as he waved and headed to his boat moored at the familiar slip. "You knew he was coming into town, you knew he was here and you didn't tell me?" Mikhail sighed with relief, then sat down, but said nothing. "You knew I applied for his foundation's grant. Doesn't family loyalty mean anything to you? They're scheduled to make their decision soon. His being here could mean that I'm a finalist for the grant, so what I want to know is this: Why didn't you think to tell me that he's been here for a week and a half?"

"Good morning, Gnat," Mikhail said politely, reminding her of the manners she'd obviously forgotten. "How are you and the boys? I'm fine. Thanks for asking."

"Don't 'Good morning, Gnat' me. I'm furious with you. And stop calling me that. I'm not that little girl buzzing around her older brothers and cousin anymore."

"I can see that," he said, sipping his coffee calmly.

"Well?" she asked, looking around his office then out the huge hurricane-glass window behind his desk. Even in her angry state, the spectacular waterfront view took her breath away. The small private marina was a panorama of serene pleasure.

Mikhail was a man of leisure most days, or that's how it appeared to outsiders. His office was in the crow's nest atop his home. He owned a small compound of oceanfront bungalows nestled around a lush serenity garden and a private beach. He also owned several high-end tour and fishing boats moored on his private docks.

"Well, what?" he asked, seriously bewildered.

"Well, is he really here about the foundation grant or what?"

He shrugged. "I have no idea."

She exhaled loudly. "The newspaper entertainment section this morning said that he's been moored here at the docks for the past week and a half. If he's here about the grant, what took him so long to find me?"

"Contrary to what others believe, I'm not totally privy to everything my patrons do while they're here in Key West. As for David Montgomery's yacht, it left port early this morning."

"But I just saw him at Nikita's place. I'm supposed to have a meeting with him this afternoon," she said exasperatedly.

"Whoa, whoa, calm down," he said, holding his hands up in surrender. "Sit, relax, chill." He got up and poured hot tea into a cup from a carafe on his credenza and offered it to her. "Here, have some chamomile tea. I know it's your favorite." She looked at the cup of tea, refusing to touch it, so he sat it on the desk in front of her. "Okay, I can see how you might be upset by all this."

"Don't try to placate me with tea and banal euphemisms."

"I wouldn't do that," he said.

"And don't patronize me, either." She glared at him for a moment then collapsed into the chair. A few seconds later she took the tea, blew gently and sipped. The hot liquid eased down her throat as the spicy sweet aroma seemed to calm her. She sighed loudly. "I'm sorry. I'm just so tired and anxious. The center's funding from the city and state fell through."

"Nat, if the center needs additional funding, why didn't you just say so? I can…" he began as he opened his center drawer and pulled out his oversize checkbook.

"No, absolutely not. I'm not taking money from my family," she insisted.

"But you obviously need it."

"Yes, I do. But I'll find a way to get it."

"Stressing yourself isn't going to change anything. I know how much you want the teen center to succeed, and I know how much you love your work. Now, the reason I didn't tell you that David Montgomery has been in Key West for the past two weeks is because he hasn't been. His assistant and his yacht were here. He only arrived recently. Apparently, he's been doing a lot of traveling. He's here on personal business and asked for my discretion. He wanted privacy and I gave him my word." She nodded. His reasoning was irrefutable. Once Mikhail Coles gave his word, it was binding. "Okay?" he asked. Natalia looked at her brother suspiciously, deciphering his exact wording. "Okay?" he repeated, expecting an affirmative answer from her.

"Do you know why he's here?"

"No."

"But he's here for a reason, correct?"

"Yes."

"And that reason involves me?"

He paused a moment. "I wasn't specifically aware of that. Are you sure?"

"No. But it seems that way. And you know nothing about it?"

"No, nothing," he said honestly. "Are we finished with the third degree or is there more?"

She paused a few seconds and pursed her lips purposely. "We'll see," she said evasively.

"And stop trying to psych me out. It's not going to work," he said.

She smiled. He knew her tricks all too well. Even before she became a family psychologist with the police, she had an uncanny way of looking deeper and seeing in people what others usually missed.

"You're just lucky I'm not still armed as a deputy sheriff or I'd have winged you when I first saw that photo of David Montgomery in the newspaper this morning," Natalia joked.

"I'll bet you would have. But then you'd have to answer to Granddad and the rest of the family."

"Believe me, I'd be doing everybody a favor," she teased. He chuckled in response. "Still, you should have told me that he was in town. And, yes, before you say anything, I know that you have celebrities coming here all the time and you never divulge that they're here, but I *am* your sister and…"

"It's what I do, Nat—discretion above all. You know that. Now, if you'll excuse me, a certain international singing sensation and a very well-known political guest will be checking in and I'd rather you not be around when they do."

"Who are they?" she joked, knowing he'd never tell.

"Come on, get out of here. I need to get back to work. How are my nephews?"

"Fine, and getting bigger, but then you wouldn't know that since you haven't been around in a few weeks." She stood and walked with her brother to the office door, then down to her car.

"Do me a favor and tell them that Uncle Mikhail's gonna stop by and take them out this weekend."

"Sounds good, but you'll have to pick them up at Stephen and Mia's place. They're babysitting this weekend," Natalia said.

"Why? Where are you going?"

"Nowhere special. I'm going to catch up on some paperwork, then paint the kitchen on Saturday. Niki and I are talking about hanging out on Sunday, but we'll see."

"So Mia and Stephen volunteered to babysit, huh?"

"Yep. They asked if they could have the boys this weekend. I said yes. But if I didn't know any better I'd say they were in parenthood practice mode."

"You think so?" Mikhail asked.

"Anything's possible, right?"

They talked a few more minutes, then his cell phone rang and he answered. He said yes, nodded a few times, glanced away and then looked back at her just before ending the call.

"I need to get back to work," he said, then kissed her cheek.

Natalia nodded. "Sure, okay. I'll catch up with you later." She waved as he quickly headed back to his office. Smiling, she shook her head. Mikhail was so predictable, but there was no way she was just going to let it go, as he'd suggested. Plus, his lame assertion that the yacht left this morning was pathetic. Of course he'd never lie to her, so she was sure that the yacht did

indeed leave, but he never said that David Montgomery
was on it.

She smiled as she got into her car and headed back
to town. She had a full day's work to complete before
four o'clock.

Chapter 5

Natalia had a hundred things to do and only a few hours to get them done. Still, she managed to arrive at the Keys Gateway Hotel ten minutes early. She walked in, stood in the massive marble lobby and gathered her thoughts. She was nervous, and few things made her nervous. Apparently, meeting with David again was one of them. She stopped at the front desk and asked for his room. The clerk called his suite, then escorted her to a separate bank of keyed elevators. He pressed a button then stepped out, allowing the doors to close with her inside. As soon as the elevator doors opened again, a petite woman with a cropped pixie haircut and a crooked smile eyed her suspiciously.

"Ms. Coles?" the woman asked. Natalia nodded. "My name is Pamela Ray. I'm David's personal assistant. I'll take you to his suite now." She stepped into the elevator beside her, inserted a key and then pressed a button to the penthouse suite.

"I read your proposal. It's very ambitious. You have some really good ideas. I could have seriously used a program like that when I was growing up in Compton, in L.A."

"Thank you. I'm proud of the program and extremely excited about the possibility of expanding the center."

"Is that all?" Pamela asked.

"Yes," Natalia answered, curious about the odd question.

"Then I'm sure it'll happen."

"I hope so," Natalia said cautiously, while wondering if everyone associated with Tinseltown was short a few lightbulbs.

The doors slid open a few seconds later. Pamela got out and walked to one of the two double-door suites on that floor. She slid a key card through the narrow slot then escorted Natalia inside. David was sitting on the sofa on his cell phone, surrounded by a number of paperbound booklets. He looked up and smiled as soon as they entered and ended his call a few seconds later.

"Thank you, Ms. Coles, for meeting me. Please, come in," he said. "May I offer you a refreshment? Coffee or tea, perhaps? Pam, would you get Ms. Coles something from the food bar?"

"No, I'm fine. Thank you," Natalia said easily as Pamela walked over to the sofa and began going through the piled booklets on the coffee table.

"Did you receive my flowers?" David asked.

"Yes, I did. Thank you. They were beautiful, but unnecessary."

"Actually, they were. I needed to apologize for my behavior yesterday. I was jet-lagged and exhausted. I wasn't quite myself."

"And who are you now?" she asked. Pamela chuckled.

David smiled. He was beginning to enjoy her quick wit. "I suppose I deserved that."

"Yes, you did."

"All's forgiven, then?" he offered with his hand extended to shake. She nodded, shaking his hand and feeling that something more was passing between them. "Please have a seat," he said to Natalia. "We'll get started in a few minutes." Natalia nodded and sat down to wait as David and Pamela finished their business.

"Is this the pile you want to consider?" Pamela asked.

"Yes. You can send the others back. I'm not interested."

"What about these two scripts?" Pamela asked.

"I'm undecided. You can leave them here for the time being and I'll read through them again. Maybe something will hit me on the second read."

With her arms loaded down, Pamela looked around and then back at David. "Is that it?"

He nodded. "That's it."

"Okay. You have an early morning publicity call for an AM talk show and a few radio call-ins after that. They're all standard, so no big deal on content. Oh, and don't forget to look over the contracts Lenny sent over. He needs them back ASAP. I'll express mail them tomorrow." He nodded on all points. "All right, that's it," Pamela said. "Have a good evening. See you later,

Ms. Coles. It was nice meeting you. Before I leave, are you sure you don't want to try the lemon-mint iced tea? It's wonderful and it comes with these pastries called Delectable Delights. They're like eating a slice of heaven."

"No, thanks," Natalia said just before Pamela left, closing the door behind her.

David walked over and sat down on the sofa beside Natalia. "So I guess we should get started," he offered. "As I said, I want to discuss your program more thoroughly. I read through the material you gave me yesterday and I have to say that I'm very impressed. You're a social worker, right?"

"Actually, I'm a family psychologist. I work with the sheriff's office and volunteer part-time at the hospital. That's how I came up with the idea for this program. Hopefully this will lead to more programs so more children won't continue to slip through the cracks."

"That's very admirable, but putting something like this together is going to take a lot of work and dedication. What does your husband think about this?"

"I'm not married, if that's what you want to know."

"But you do have a child?"

"Yes, I have two boys. One is three years old and the other is nine months old. Is that going to be a problem?" she asked defensively.

"It depends. I've seen personal concerns become increasingly distracting and eventually have a detrimental effect on a potentially gifted career. It would be disappointing to see a very promising program fail because of personal issues."

"Not with me."

He shrugged. "It's just that you mentioned that you have plans this evening and I just want to make sure that the gentleman friend with whom you're dining understands the commitment involved."

"I assure you, that's not an issue and if you want to know anything more about my personal life and with whom I dine, just come right out and ask me. Getting this grant is important to me and if answering these questions will help, I'm happy to do it." She watched him almost smile, revealing he'd been found out. "I'm sorry, I thought you were serious about this project."

"I *am* serious," he affirmed, his expression hardening again. "The question is, Ms. Coles, are you? Can you handle putting this together plus everything else?"

"Without a doubt," she said.

"Excellent, then we're on the same page," he said, watching as she tilted her head knowingly. "You're very intuitive."

"And you're very perceptive."

"My foundation's credibility is on the line here," he said.

"Correction. *Children's lives are on the line here.*"

He nodded, conceding her point. "You do speak your mind, don't you? I like that."

She nodded then pulled out her notes, a leather-bound ledger and the proposal. "Shall we get started?" They began and talked for nearly an hour, exchanging ideas and considering each other's suggestions. David was impressed by her focus and commitment and she was amazed that, along with his natural business sense, he seemed caring and compassionate. As they finished, she smiled to herself. He noticed.

"You're smiling. Any particular reason?"

"I guess I should apologize for calling you self-serving and narcissistic."

"You didn't call me that."

"Yes, I did. You just weren't in the car at the time. It was when I was on my way to the nursery school yesterday."

He smiled and nodded. "Touché. Speaking of which, no more emergencies with your son, I hope," he asked.

"No, he's fine. He's three and he's such a little character. If there's trouble to be gotten into, he's there."

"That sounds about right for a three-year-old," he said, thinking about some of the stories he remembered his grandmother telling about him at that age.

Natalia shook her head and smiled brightly. "He's always into something and it looks like his little brother is going to be just like him. Do you have any children?" she asked, then caught herself. "That was too personal. It's none of my business."

He wasn't prepared for her question but, always quick on his feet, he answered a split second later. "No problem. I've been around friends with kids that age. They can certainly be a handful."

She realized that he didn't answer her direct question, but she let it go, assuming that stars of his caliber preferred to keep their personal life, well, personal. "It looks like we're done here," she said. "Or is there something else you'd like to know?"

"Actually, I'd like you to tell me more about yourself. Excuse the expression, but when doing business I like to know exactly who and what kind of person I'm getting into bed with."

"I understand completely. What do you want to know?"

"Whatever you'd like to tell me."

"Okay, I'm twenty-nine years old. I worked as a deputy sheriff while I was getting my psychology degree. I'm an excellent marksperson. I'm currently a psychologist and social worker working with my grandfather, the sheriff. And I guess that's it."

"Not quite. You're intelligent, insightful, poised and disciplined. You apparently have a huge heart when it comes to children. And you're also very beautiful."

"Thank you," she said softly.

"You're welcome," he replied as a tense moment passed between them. It seemed like the air around them was suddenly charged with electricity. "Tell me about your family."

"My mother and father live here in Florida. I have two sisters: Nikita, a pastry chef whom you met, and Tatiana, a news correspondent in London. I also have two brothers: Dominik is a doctor and Mikhail owns a small business on the docks. I'm the middle child. What about you? I obviously know your onscreen persona, but what about the real you?"

"Fair enough. I'm thirty-two years old. I was born and raised in Compton, California, surrounded by gangs, drugs, prostitution—you name it. I never knew my father. My sister and I were raised by my mother." He stopped. There was no way he was going to tell her the whole truth.

"You have a sister?" she asked with added interest.

He nodded. "She was six years younger than me. She was brilliant—way smarter than me. I took care of her as we were growing up. Then I turned my back for a second and she was gone. She was killed years ago, before any of this happened."

"I'm sorry," she said softly, sensing his anguish. Instinctively, she reached out and gripped his hand. "You know, she would be very proud of you right now. Everything you've accomplished is obviously a testament to your love for her and your devotion to her memory. Your career, your foundation, the people you've helped all attest to that."

He nodded as he looked at Natalia, smiling. No one had ever said that to him before. It felt good because in his heart he knew it was true. Brenda *would* have been very proud of him.

"Thank you for saying that."

"You're welcome," she said. "It's true."

"She would have liked you."

They looked into each other's eyes and a sudden urge enveloped them. It was the same urge that had been simmering just below the surface since the moment they met. This could change everything. They both felt it and they both knew it. Both had risks. She knew he'd break her heart. He knew that with one phone call, she could shatter his world. Still, the foregone conclusion was in their eyes. It was going to happen; the only question was when. She backed off first.

"Well, I guess that's it. I should go now," she said quickly, hoping to defuse the tenseness surrounding them.

"I'll need this proposal revised to include what we

talked about today. Also, I'd like to see your primary location and a list of contractors you're considering for the expansion. This has to be completely up to code, no shortcuts," he said. She nodded while continuing to take notes. "We'll also need my foundation's legal team to look this over for particulars after it's complete. The foundation will be meeting in the early part of next month. If you miss that window, you'll have to wait until next year. I'll be away for the next few days. Do you think you can put all this together by then?"

"Sure, no problem," she affirmed.

"You can do all that? Sounds like you're Wonder Woman."

"Nah, I'm a just a single mom—the next best thing."

He smiled, impressed by her can-do attitude and confidence. "A single mom as Wonder Woman, huh," he said.

"That's right. Didn't you know that single moms can leap tall building blocks, fly from school to soccer practice like a bird, plus do a tub of laundry, cook macaroni and cheese and read a bedtime story in a single day?"

He chuckled. "No, guess I missed that memo."

She smiled, knowing that he was thinking about his mother. "Some of us just do what we need to do—no apologies, no excuses and no regrets. We do it for our children."

"And what about a male influence?" he asked.

Her expression changed as she glanced away. Then a split second later she smiled and looked him directly in the eye. "My sons have everything they need. If they need a man's influence later on, then I'll call on my dad, my grandfather, my brothers and my cousins."

"But not their father?" he pushed further.

"No, not their father," she answered assertively.

"Why not?" he pressed. "There had to be a father."

"Not in this case. There is a biological donor—that's it."

"That sounds pretty sterile, impersonal."

"Is this still part of the 'know who you're in bed with' interview?"

"No," he said, backing off slightly, seeing that she was more uncomfortable than before. "It's just me. I'm always curious about relationships and the choices people make."

"I see. Okay, well, my decision—sterile and impersonal as it seems—was made because I love children and I wanted my own. Waiting around for Mr. Right or Prince Charming isn't my style."

"You're a beautiful woman, any man would be crazy not to…"

"Okay. This is just weird. I'm sitting here chatting with a mega movie star about my sex life—or lack thereof."

"Lack thereof?" he questioned quickly. She didn't reply. He shrugged. "I'm just saying that it appears the men around here are obviously not paying attention to the rare beauty in their midst. I am. So maybe I'm not completely rude or crazy after all," he suggested, alluding to their first meeting in her office.

"It's easy to forget that you're a consummate actor," Natalia commented. "If I didn't know any better, I'd think you were actually flirting with me."

"You can't tell for sure? I must be slipping," he joked.

She took a deep breath and sighed slowly. "It's a good thing you're leaving soon."

"Trying to get rid of me already?" he said with a twinkle in his eye.

"No, not at all. On the contrary, you're dangerous to a woman's heart. Oh, and you forgot—overmedicated."

"That's right. I forgot about that little gem." He chuckled, remembering their first conversation. "You're good. I like that."

"Do you?" she asked.

"Yeah, I do. A lot."

They paused a moment, looking into each other's eyes again. There was definitely something there—an attraction and an easy compatibility that was relaxed and comfortable. It was as if there was more to everything they said and did than the surface veneer. "Okay. Getting back to you telling me more about your life?"

"Boring, believe me." He quickly glanced at his watch. "It's getting late, so maybe we can…"

"Oh, right. Sorry," she interrupted quickly. "You probably have plans this evening and I must be encroaching on someone else's time. I'd better go."

"No, don't. What I was going to say—actually ask— was if you'd like to join me for dinner this evening."

"To continue talking about the project?" she asked as she began gathering her notes, folders and other information.

"I think we have that pretty well taken care of, don't you think?"

"So you mean join you for dinner—talking-and-just-hanging-out dinner?" she clarified. He nodded. "That's very tempting, but probably not a good idea."

"Ah, right. *Your* dinner date," he said.

"For the record, you assume it's a date. I said that I had dinner plans. My plans are hanging out with my sons tonight."

"Yes, Supermom. But doesn't being Supermom limit your social life?"

She chuckled. "That would assume that I have a social life," she joked. "Truthfully, I don't think I'm missing much." She stood to put some distance between them.

He stood and stepped closer. "I wouldn't say that."

"Dinner, a movie, bowling—what else am I missing?"

"I can think of one thing."

"What?" she asked.

"This…" He leaned in and tipped her chin up closer to his mouth. She opened her mouth to speak, but found herself just holding her breath as her heart pounded through her chest. His mouth hovered a split second before he captured hers. Their lips touched gently at first and then an explosion of passion surged.

Seldom taken off guard, Natalia was stunned, not by the kiss, but by her reaction to it. He was kissing her, and she was nearly out of control. It was like a fireball hurled at the top of a snow-covered mountain. An avalanche of desire freed itself and slammed into her full force. She wrapped her arms around his neck as he slid his arms around her waist, drawing her body closer to his. He was taking her on the ride of a lifetime. She heard herself moan from deep in her throat.

His kiss was arousing, and the spine-tingling sensation she felt was beyond anything she'd ever experienced. This wasn't just a kiss, this was a pursuit. Her heart jumped and her thoughts spun wildly. It was a headlong spiral and she was out of control.

The kiss deepened as their tongues tangled and tangoed, the familiar mating dance. The intensity grew, this time like an erupting volcano—hot, fiery and furious. Natalia was losing control. It had been too long since a man had held her in his arms like this. Now that the man kissing her was David Montgomery, it muddled her mind even more. This had to be a dream and, if it was, she never wanted to wake up. But she knew that it wasn't and that she had to stop. She leaned back, breathless, but he captured her mouth a second time. She relented eagerly, overpowered by the sensual pull they both felt. Then, finally clearing her dazed mind, she pushed back again, planting her hand firmly on his broad chest.

"…the good-night kiss," he said, continuing their conversation.

"Wait. This isn't happening," she muttered breathlessly as she felt his heart beating madly. She quickly dropped her hand and touched her swollen lips.

"But it is," he assured her, gently stroking her body.

"No, it can't be. We can't be."

"Why not?" he asked ardently. "When was the last time you lost control and allowed passion to rule?"

"Never."

"That's far too long."

"You—you don't belong here and I do. Our worlds

are a million light-years apart. They don't even come close to meshing."

"But we do mesh, don't we? I feel it and you feel it, too."

She saw his eyes twinkle and seem to spark. She shook her head, smiling, then swallowed hard. "You're good, very good."

"Yes, I am."

She looked into his soulful eyes. She did feel it. She knew deep in her heart that they had connected. Something—she couldn't say what—was pulling them, pushing them. But this wasn't what she needed right now. Her life was complicated enough without adding a movie star to the mix. "David, we have nothing in common and you will most certainly break my heart."

"We have this," he said, leaning in and kissing her again.

Her body melted against his. It had been such a long time and it felt so good to be held. She never wanted this to end, but she knew it was impossible. She pushed back, breathless. "I can't." She shook her head. "No, I can't be here right now. I can't do the one-night-stand thing," she said, stepping back.

"Who says this is a one-night stand?"

"Are you acting now?"

"No," he said truthfully, surprising himself.

She looked into his eyes, seeing sincerity, but that didn't change what was going on between them. She stepped up and kissed him tenderly, then allowed herself one last fantasy as she closed her eyes and leaned against his chest. He held her a brief moment, then she looked up at him. "I can't do this. You are too tempting and I can't jeopardize everything I've worked for," she said as she pushed back again. "I need to go now." She picked up her things and walked to the door. Turning just once, she looked at him standing there. She smiled and shook her head. "I must be insane. I just turned David Montgomery down." She opened the door and left.

David had to smile as he watched her leave. He wanted her now more than ever. Any other woman would have jumped at the opportunity to be in his bed tonight, but she didn't. That in itself was unprecedented. But he found it encouraging. She wasn't like every other woman. He picked up the proposal and flipped through, seeing her smiling face on the bio page. He had a feeling of warmth that he hadn't known in a long time.

Chapter 6

The next day a large bouquet of flowers arrived by special delivery. The note was simple. It thanked her for their evening together then told her to miss him and keep busy while he was away. With that note, the sudden reality of the situation hit home, causing her concern. What was she about to get herself into? He flirted—yes, he kissed her—yes, he seemed to want more—yes, and heaven help her, she did, too. She wanted him. There was no getting around it. She rationalized loneliness, sexual frustration, curiosity, admiration, but the truth was simpler. He'd gotten to her as no one else had.

She knew this was all fantasy. *He* was fantasy. Nothing was real in his life, but hers was grounded in reality. She had a family and responsibilities. Rationalizing or not, she knew she had to set her desires aside and focus on channeling her energy to those who needed her. But still the image of their kiss overshadowed her dreams both day and night. It was more than attraction; it was enticement, and he was temptation personified.

She'd walked away that evening; it was the hardest thing she'd done in a long time, but she'd known she had to. That night, after she put her sons to bed, she dreamt that she and David were making love and all night long she tossed and turned, imagining her body on top then intertwined with his. Hard, firm and writhing, she fantasized about feeling him deep inside her. She awoke wet and breathless.

The man was incredible. Just ten minutes in his arms and he'd given her a burning fever that days later she still couldn't forget. It was more than movie-star magnetism or charisma. When he looked at her, she felt as if he was seeing into her soul. It was as if a part of him had seeped into her heart and no matter what she did, or where she was, she felt him. He was part of her—there was no denying it.

Three days passed. The local newspaper reported that Key West's newest celebrity resident was out of town, but would be back. Of course, she already knew that. She'd skillfully tucked him away as a fond memory and gone back to her real life. Thankfully, she had her sons, her work and the center to keep her busy. Still, she'd suddenly see him wherever she turned—on early-morning talk shows, late-night talk shows and everywhere in between. Once, when cleverly asked about his current fascination with Key West, he smiled and said that he was just there for rest and relaxation. The Key West newspapers clamored to get the latest scoop on the newest celeb in their midst.

Flowers arrived the fourth day without a note,

although she knew they were from him. Late Friday evening she was in her office, busy finalizing a foster care placement, when she heard a knock on the door. With the door partially open, she looked up, seeing David smiling that smile. "Miss me?" he asked.

She smiled and sat back in her chair nonchalantly. "Hardly. You're not the only superstar actor in my life," she joked.

"Oh, really," he said curiously as he walked into her office. "Who stopped by? Anyone I know?"

"No, you don't. My son Brice is in the nursery school play next week. He's portraying a tree and the critics agree that he's brilliant," she said as only a proud mother could. "I just got back from watching rehearsals."

David went still and his expression was telling. The sudden realization of his son onstage slammed into him hard. *His son onstage*—the monumental implication of that had floored him. There was a scramble of emotion surging through him. He was proud and thrilled and it was obvious that his feelings were getting more and more convoluted. His heart wanted to reach out, but he knew he couldn't, not yet.

"He's so excited," she continued. "Of course he has no concept of time, so when I told him that the play is next week, he thought it was today. And, of course, Jayden wants to get into the act. They're so adorable together… Hey, are you okay? You look a bit shell-shocked."

The consummate actor quickly stepped back into character. "I'm fine, just jet-lagged again. I've been flying all over the country."

"Yes, I've seen you. Morning shows, late-night talk shows, New York, L.A., Houston, Chicago."

"It's all busywork. Speaking of which, are you busy tonight?" he asked.

"Not really, why?"

"I have some ideas that I'd like to run by you."

"Great, I have a few minutes. Can we do it now?" she asked.

"Can't, I've got a radio interview to do in a few minutes. This evening would be better. How about a working dinner?" he suggested.

"Fine. I'll meet you at…"

"Why don't I pick you up at your house?" he said, quickly cutting her off before she finished.

"This isn't a date. You don't have to pick me up," she said.

"I'd like to."

"Speaking of which, how did you get my home address to send the flowers?" she asked.

"My assistant is very good at what she does. I'll send a driver to pick you up at your home at six. See you then."

She stood quickly, intending to decline the ride, but he was already out the door. She sat back down, knowing this was trouble. Thinking about him constantly was one thing, being with him again was going to be impossible. She glanced at the photos of her sons on her desk and smiled. They were her center. Seeing them proved that she could do anything. Yes. She could do this. If it was dinner at the hotel restaurant, she'd enjoy it like any other dinner out. If it was served in his suite, she'd keep the conversation focused on the teen center, his foundation and their work together. There—she was pleased with her strategy. It was an infallible plan.

The car arrived at 5:45 p.m. She was ready. She'd chosen to wear evening casual, an emerald-green, sleeveless, knee-length wrap dress with a softly ruffled collar. It plunged slightly lower in front than she'd intended, but it was simple and elegant. She chose taupe-colored, four-inch stiletto heels and carried a matching handbag. As the car drove off, she turned and looked back at the empty house. Stephen and Mia had already picked up the boys at the nursery school. As of right now, she was a free woman—at least for the next two days.

The black sedan drove through the center of Key West then continued on. She looked out the window, knowing that if they were going to have dinner at the hotel the driver was most definitely lost. "Excuse me," she began. "Aren't we going to the Keys Gateway Hotel?"

The driver looked up at her in the rearview mirror. "No, ma'am. My instructions are to deliver you to the docks by six-twenty."

She nodded. "Thank you." She sat back, wondering where they were going to dine. There were any number of elegant restaurants on the pier. A few minutes later she was surprised to see that the car pulled into her brother's private parking lot. It stopped just as David was walking down from the pier. He smiled as he opened the door and extended his hand to her. She got out and his eyes instantly roamed all over her.

"You look stunning," he said.

"Thank you. You look pretty nice yourself," she said admiringly. He wore a dark blue jacket, tan pants and a dark blue, striped, button-down shirt topped with dark sunglasses and a summer trilby hat. "Where are we dining?" she asked.

"I thought it would be nice to take the boat out. I have an excellent chef on board and perhaps we can cruise along the coast later this evening."

"That sounds great," she said cautiously. This wasn't part of her plan.

He tipped his elbow to her and escorted her down the wooden pier toward his yacht. It was much larger and grander than she'd expected. He walked the narrow plank, stepped on board, then reached back to take her hand and help her as she followed. "Welcome aboard," David said.

"Thank you." Natalia stepped onto a deck of pure opulence. She looked around slowly, taking in the beauty of her surroundings. "Wow, this is awesome."

"It's comfortable," he said.

"More than comfortable, I'd say. You live here?"

"It solves the whole privacy issue. The media and paparazzi would have to go through a lot to get to me here."

"Paranoid about your privacy?" she asked.

"Believe me, there's nothing paranoid about it. In my world, you're hounded day and night for a brief glimpse into your life. Celebrity photos go for thousands of dollars. The incentive to cash in is tremendous. The simplest daily action can become fodder for a tabloid front-page story. Sometimes it's impossible to have any semblance of an ordinary life."

"Is that what you want—an ordinary life? Somehow I don't see you with a wife, two kids, a dog and a white picket fence."

"Maybe not the white picket fence part," he said, smiling.

She nodded, taking his word for it. "So for the time being you just sail around, going from place to place?"

"Sometimes, but usually it's docked in St. Croix. I have a house there. It's quiet and peaceful. I spend most of my time there, studying, when I'm not filming. Come on, I'll show you around."

He started the tour on the flybridge then walked across to the top sundeck. There was a large Jacuzzi with surrounding lounge chairs and a side bar. On the other side were two Jet Skis and beyond that a small dinghy. She paused a moment to lean against the side rail. "So, you mentioned that you study. Study what?"

"Lines and scripts, mostly," he said, leaning back beside her. "Sometimes I study character patterns and research motivations and development."

She turned to him. "That's right. Sometimes I forget that you're a famous mega movie star. I guess it's because you just don't seem like it. You're just a regular guy."

"I am and I take that as a compliment."

"So are you getting ready to make another movie?" she asked as they continued walking, returning to the upper deck area. They went into his study, then a small game room with pool table.

"Yes. Production was pushed back. Now it starts in a few months. That's what I was doing when you stopped by the other day. I was going though the script again and also looking through others."

"You're looking at *more* scripts?"

He nodded. "Always. I get about ten scripts a week."

"Wow. So people just send them directly to you?"

"No, most are given to my agent from studio development. My agent reads them, then sends the more promising ones to me. Pam goes through them and then I see them."

"And Pamela is your personal assistant."

"Yes, I've known Pam since forever. She was my sister's best friend for years growing up. She was there when Brenda died. I've kind of taken care of her since then. I put her through college and she goes wherever I go."

He slid a door aside and they walked into the most exquisite lounge she had ever seen. "This is the salon." Natalia stepped inside and removed her sunglasses. Italian black marble and red mahogany were a part of everything. Two oversize cream-colored sofas, a huge plasma TV, inset lighting, plush carpeting—it was all magnificent.

In front of the main seating area was an intimate dining space with a double-pedestal table set for two. She walked over, speechless by the splendor. The centerpiece flowers and lit candle made the crystal glassware shimmer and sparkle. The delicate china, with David's initials stamped on the rim, completed the fine table arrangement. "This is magnificent."

David removed his jacket, sunglasses and trilby, then stopped at the built-in bar. He opened a bottle of champagne and carried over two glasses. After filling both glasses and giving one to her, he held his glass up to toast. "To you, Natalia Coles, an amazing Wonder Woman."

"Thank you." She nodded her acceptance.

"So how about going for a ride along the coast?"

"That would be nice."

He picked up the phone on the bar and told the captain to take them for a short ride. A few minutes later, she heard the soft hum of the engine and felt the gentle forward motion of the vessel. There was a knock on the door as it opened slightly. David turned and nodded. A steward rolled in a tray with several covered domes. "Perfect timing." He turned to her. "Dinner is ready."

The meal was exceptional and the conversation was enjoyable. They had lobster and crab medallions in a rich creamy butter sauce with baked potato and spring green salad. Each mouthful was a delectable delicacy of pure delight. Over dinner they talked about his movie career and what it was like on the set of a major motion picture. She was surprised by the antics and playfulness he confessed participating in while on the set. When dessert arrived, they talked about his many travels. The French chocolate mousse imperial was luscious and mouthwatering. While they ate he told her all about Italy, Prague, Asia, Mongolia and New Zealand, to name just a few.

After dessert they moved back to the salon area and sat sipping champagne and eating cheese and melon slices. They talked about their lives and careers, and for the next hour and a half simply enjoyed being together. "Come on. Let's go outside and get some air." They stepped on deck just as the sun was setting. The sky was a fiery red against the water's blue horizon.

"You know all this is wasted on me, right?" she said.

"All what?" he asked.

"The ambience, soft jazz music playing inside, gentle waves lapping the hull, smooth swaying motion, the candles, the champagne, the soft lighting and, of course, the sun setting on cue."

"I don't know what you mean," he confessed innocently.

"Okay, mister. You may star in the movies, but I've seen a few in my day. This is Seduction 101."

He laughed. "I assure you this isn't a seduction scene. Your virtue is relatively safe with me."

She nodded, smiling, as they both turned to witness the last of the sun dip over the horizon. The muted hum of the engine and the lapping of waves seemed to slow everything down. Natalia stared out, seeing more than just the vast water around them. She saw possibilities, the future. Everything she'd always wanted was within her reach. She had her family, her friends and her career. She had everything any woman could want except…

"Where are you?" David asked, moving close, seeing her lost in her thoughts. Natalia turned to him, questioning. "You look like you're miles away," he added.

"Sorry, I was just thinking."

"Your sons?" he asked. She nodded. "Where are they this evening?"

"My cousin and his wife asked if they could baby-sit this weekend. Actually, I think the request was orchestrated by the rest of my family to give me a break. But I miss them. This is the first time in a long time that we've been apart. I know it's only been a few hours, but still, it feels strange."

"I guess it's not as easy as you thought, being a single mom."

"It's challenging. I'm sure you remember what your mom went through, constant worry and endless concern when the children are out of your sight."

"Actually, my mother wasn't exactly the mother-of-the-year type. My sister and I were in her way most of the time. All she cared about was men, money and pursuing her own pleasure. After a while, she dumped us off at her sister's house and never looked back. Then we were shuttled from one relative to another—anyone who would take us."

"That's not how it's supposed to be," she said sadly.

"You're right, it's not. Question: any regrets?"

"You mean about having Brice and Jayden?" she asked. He nodded. "No, never. They're my heart. I look at them and I see love, joy and perfection. They're innocent and free and curious, and I love them beyond measure. You'll see one day when you have children. There's nothing like that feeling. When you first look into their eyes and see yourself, your heart instantly opens and love pours out. After that, you're forever full of love, even when they're driving you crazy."

"And you don't know anything about the father?"

"He was a number—that's all."

"Is that what you're going to tell your sons?"

She took a deep breath and released it slowly. "Truthfully, I don't know what I'm going to tell them when the time comes. But they will know that they are loved and wanted—that much I can say for sure." She turned away as troubling thoughts seeped into her mind. His question was valid—she'd asked herself the same thing dozens of times, even before she had the first procedure. But her love always won out.

David saw her withdraw and sensed that she was disheartened. "So when do I get to meet the two budding stage stars?" he asked, turning to her.

"Probably not a good idea," she said cautiously. Then, seeing his disappointment, she continued. "It's not you, David. It's a rule I have about people in their lives. They're too young to understand that you won't always be around. They get attached quickly and easily. If they meet you, they'll want to see you the next day and the day after that and so on."

"I understand, and agree," he said. "So tell me about dating and relationships for you."

"I'm so busy I don't have time to even think about dating."

"Now that is truly sad," he said with a smile.

"I'm serious. I have so much going on in my life right now that all I can do is concentrate on my sons and my work. What about you? How much dating do you do?" she asked.

"That's different," he protested. "My life and my career are..."

"Crazy, busy, distracting, demanding, hectic?" she offered.

"Definitely," he said.

"Ah, but still you take the time to date, right?"

"Okay, point taken. But it seems that neither of us has taken the time to explore a serious relationship," he said.

"Oh, come on. You expect me to buy that? There are literally thousands of women dying to meet you and another hundred thousand who wouldn't mind dating you. And I'm not even counting the rich, the super-rich, actresses and models."

He laughed. "And you think they would interest me?"

"Darling, they would interest about eighty-five percent of the male population on this planet, so why not you?"

"No offense to the thousands of women clamoring for my attention, but my taste is a bit more discriminating. I've had too many outrageous experiences with pampered and privileged women."

"Still, you have models and starlets dropping at your feet."

"Come here." He smiled, grabbed her and wrapped his arm around her waist, affectionately drawing her flush against his hard body. Taken by surprise, Natalia gasped and clutched on to his forearms as she leaned against his body. She looked up into his eyes and relaxed instantly. It felt so good to rest against him and to be in his arms.

"Know this, Natalia Coles. You are the first woman I've wanted to be out with in a very, very long time. For me, dating is complicated at best. I'm not going to lie to you: it's flattering to have women throwing themselves at me. There will always be starlets, groupies and models around me. But I know what's important in my life and being here right now with you is important to me. This is where I want to be."

She looked into his eyes and saw sincerity, but that

wasn't enough. She shook her head. "What are we doing here, David? What am *I* doing here?" she asked. "I don't belong here. Your life isn't normal; mine is. I'm a mom and a social worker, hardly a glamorous…"

"You're a beautiful, desirable woman and so much more—more, in fact, than you even know."

She was speechless. It wasn't the flattery. It was the genuineness that touched her. She'd had attractive men in her life before. Successful, wealthy and charming, but none of them even compared to David. He was everything any woman could ever want and right now he was here with her, wanted to be with her, and she knew that she wanted him. And that alone scared her. "You are a consummate actor. Still, I thank you for the compliment. But that doesn't answer my question."

"What are we doing here together?" he guessed. She nodded. "I don't know. I do know that I find myself liking you more than I imagined. I'm enjoying myself and I have been since meeting you. You draw people in and make them feel special, at ease. I can't think of any other place I want to be except right here, right now talking with you, being with you. You're not the person I expected to find."

She waited to respond because it seemed that he wanted to say more, but for some reason didn't or couldn't. "Thank you," she said as she stepped out of his embrace to lean on the rail again. "You know, to tell you the truth, I'm a little starstruck being here with you."

"I'm not that guy. They're just roles I play on-screen."

"I know. Still, being here just talking is so...
strange."

"Strange good or strange bad?" he asked.

She looked at him and smiled. "Strange very good,"
she clarified.

"I'm delighted to hear that." He took a step closer,
guiding her back into his arms. She went willingly as
he cupped her face in his hands. The space between
their bodies vanished and the air around them went still.
Their eyes held a moment as he took the opportunity to
trail his finger over her lips. Her heart thundered and
her stomach fluttered. She knew he was going to kiss
her again and she knew that she would willingly accept.
He nodded slowly. She nodded, as well, then tipped her
head upward as he leaned in.

Soft and tender at first, his mouth touched hers. Then
over and over again, he kissed her. Eyes closed, heads
turning slowly with each kiss, mouths parted, the kisses
continued until finally he wrapped her in his arms and
captured her mouth with fierce purpose.

Her lips parted and he delved deep into her mouth.
She swam in the deliciousness of him, wanting even
more. Their tongues danced, savoring the last remnants
of champagne and the sweet nectar of desire. The
sensation was mind-blowing. Her thoughts delighted in
endless pleasure. Her passion and hunger surged as her
unrestrained arousal soared. Like lava burning down the
side of a mountain, her body was ablaze, molten both
inside and out. She'd never felt this intense stirring before.
It was all-consuming, penetrating every part of her body.
One kiss, one perfect kiss, and he'd set her on fire.

Her body was hot, his body was hard. A delectable

myriad of sensations swirled all around her. His taste was intoxicating, his scent was exhilarating and the feel of his body so hard and arousing was staggering. Even the sounds around her were intense—music, soft at first, then louder and clearer as her thoughts slowly eased through the haze of longing that surrounded her. The kiss ended and the music continued. Then it hit her: it wasn't music; it was her cell phone.

"I need to get that," she said breathlessly, stepping away. Hearing the cell phone chime, he instantly released her. He nodded and watched as she hurried back into the salon to get her purse. When she was out of view, he turned back to the rail and looked out at the gulf. Thankfully, the deepening darkness hid the distressed expression on his face. He knew that Natalia's question was valid. What were they doing here? This—all this— was getting way out of control. The simple plan he had formulated to find out the kind of woman she was had turned into something else entirely.

He was getting too involved, but he couldn't help himself. When they were apart she was all he could think about. At first he thought it was merely because she was the mother of his two sons, but now he knew different. It wasn't the fear of what she could do to him and his career. It was the fear of not being with her again. In an instant he knew that she had gotten to that tiny part of his heart that he'd always kept sealed off.

Wanting her was natural. He was a man and she was an attractive woman. Being with her was also easy. She was a caring and compassionate person with a tender heart and an open spirit. Kissing her was the problem. He enjoyed it too much. He glanced back briefly, hearing her sweet laughter, then turned to look out into the gathering darkness again.

The question wasn't what they doing here. The question was what was *he* doing here? He knew there were a hundred reasons why he should just drop her off on the dock, turn and keep going, but the pull inside wouldn't let him do it. All he had to do was walk away. No one would ever know about his feelings or the children—not Natalia, not anyone. But he knew that what started as a solely selfish, protective, personal instinct had turned into something even more personal.

Inside, Natalia grabbed her purse and found her cell phone. She held it tight but didn't return the call just yet. She needed to compose herself. She took a deep breath and tried to get her wayward emotions in check. It was impossible. Her heart still pounded, and her nerve endings tingled. David was too good at unnerving her, and no matter how hard she tried to convince herself otherwise, she wanted to be with him. Not because he was who he was, but because there was something about him that drew her to him. She felt off balance, as if she were constantly falling. The thing was this: If she fell, would he be there to catch her?

Her cell rang again. She answered instantly. The conversation with the boys was short and enjoyable. It was exactly what she needed to get back to the reality of her life. Sailing beneath a starry, moonlit sky with a movie star by her side was for someone else—certainly not her. A few moments later, Natalia stepped back out onto the deck. She saw David standing where she'd left him. He stared out at the darkening sky. "I'm back," she said.

He turned, seeing her standing just beyond the doorway. The softness of her dress blew teasingly against the warm breeze as the moment sparkled in the moonlight. "Everything okay?" he asked.

She nodded and moved back to the rail beside him. "Yes, everything's great. The boys just called to say good night."

"You said they were staying with relatives, right?"

"Yes, Mia and Stephen are my cousins. They're newlyweds. I think they're considering starting a family, and having Brice and Jayden for the weekend will give them a taste of parenthood."

She paused a moment then continued. "David, thank you for tonight, I had a wonderful time. This was truly memorable."

"You're very welcome. But it doesn't have to end just yet, does it?"

"It's getting late," she said.

"But your sons are in good hands, right?" he asked. She nodded. "Great, so why don't we do something special. Let's go away, too."

"Go away? You're kidding, right?"

"No, I'm serious. We're already on the water. In a few more hours we can be in Miami, the Bahamas or even Jamaica. It'll be a mini vacation. I'm sure you could use one, couldn't you?"

She laughed, assuming that he was joking. Then she thought about her conversation with her sister. It was as if he'd been reading her thoughts. "Wait. You're serious, aren't you?" she asked.

He nodded. "Very."

"No, I can't do that," she insisted as she moved farther away, physically distancing herself from the suggestion.

"Why not? We'll go to the Bahamas and be back Sunday morning. Unless, of course, you have something planned for Saturday. Do you?" he asked, knowing she didn't after having overheard her conversation with her sister at the bakery.

"Whatever I have or don't have planned for Saturday doesn't matter. No, this is crazy. Nobody goes to the Bahamas just like that. People plan, make reservations."

"You're right. Then again, some people just sail off at sunset," he assured her.

"No, I didn't pack. I don't have anything to wear," Natalia argued.

"Don't worry about clothes. We'll pick up whatever you need when we get there."

"What about a passport? Mine's at home."

"I'm sure you have a Florida driver's license with you. That'll suffice for boat passengers at a private port like this one."

Natalia bit her lower lip. This was all beginning to sound like it could really happen. It was sudden and exciting and reminiscent of her life a long, long time ago. "No, I can't," she said quickly, resigning herself to painting and gardening.

"Are you sure?" He moved closer as he asked. "Is there any way I can get you to change your mind?"

She looked into his eyes, knowing that he saw she was tempted. "This is crazy." Natalia walked away slowly.

The temptation to do something for herself was strong. On the one hand, she had work and responsibility; on the other hand, there was David. She knew that Brice and Jayden would be fine. She thought for a half second more before she turned, smiled and answered. "Okay."

David smiled and nodded. He kissed her briefly then headed up to the flybridge. Natalia went back into the salon. She grabbed her cell phone and called Mia and Stephen again. She told them that she'd be away all day Saturday with David. Mia was overjoyed and told her that they'd planned to take the boys to the aquarium, their favorite place, and then Stephen, Mikhail and Dominik were taking Brice fishing Saturday afternoon. Jayden would stay with her. Natalia hung up knowing that everything was fine. They'd be in good hands, but she still felt the pangs of separation. She keyed up their photos on her cell phone.

"Everything all right?" David asked, walking back into the salon.

Natalia looked up and smiled. She nodded. "Yes."

"Are you sure? We can still head back if you're having second thoughts."

"No, I'm just missing my little guys. That's all," she said as she flipped to another photo.

"Is that a photo of them?" David asked, seeing the image still lit up as her cell phone wallpaper. She nodded, changed to the photo gallery and handed it to him. His heart pounded and his face lit up instantly. The first shot was them playing in water. The joyful smiles on their faces were priceless. He toggled through the rest of the photos, feeling a connection he hadn't expected and emotions he'd never felt before. "Wow, they're really handsome, aren't they?" he said, smiling.

"Yes, they are. They're both little charmers with two distinctly different personalities. Brice is the adventurous one. He's always into or up to something. I don't know what I'm gonna do when he's a teenager—probably inject him with a LoJack for teens or something like that. Jayden is more of the lover-boy type. He's such a ladies' man. Women look at him and just start drooling, and he loves it."

David chuckled, recognizing the attributes in himself.

"So, are we all set for tomorrow?" she asked, seeing his odd reaction to the photos of her sons. He nodded absently, still thinking about the photos. The feeling of pride overwhelmed him. These were his sons—happy, healthy and handsome. He thought about his own childhood and how very different it was than what they'd experience. Growing up in a loveless home without a father was no way for a child to live.

"Hey, you're a million miles away. Are you okay?" she asked.

"Yeah, I was just thinking," he said finally, handing her back the cell phone.

"It must have been something pretty emotional. The expression on your face seemed almost pained."

"Childhood," he said simply.

She leaned in and touched his arm. "We seldom get over our past. It's what makes us who we are in the present and what shapes our view of the world for our future. We are who we were. There's no getting around that. No matter how hard we try to run away from or erase the past, our experiences are always with us. But it's the experiences that we have now and the relationships that we forge now that make us who we are."

He smiled. "You're right. You're absolutely right. We are exactly who we were and it is what we do now that shapes our present and our future. You're pretty good at this psychology stuff."

"You think so, huh?"

"I know so."

"Working in social services has a way of broadening a person's view of the world. I've seen people on the worst day of their lives and also the best day. The joy I get from handing an adopted child over to her new family is pure exhilaration. And equally, the heartbreak of removing a child from an abusive family is just as exhilarating because I know that that child, even with the physical and emotional scars, will go forward to be a better person and have a better life."

"You're a remarkable woman."

"Because I work with families and children?" she asked.

"No, because you care so much and because you give your heart so willingly," he replied. "Brice and Jayden are very lucky little guys."

"Actually, I'm the lucky one. I learned so much from them. One thing is that some things you just can't control and you can't option out. Everything happens for a reason."

"Everything?" he asked, thinking about the situation that connected them, unbeknownst to her. She nodded. He turned away. If only she knew how true those words were. They stayed up talking well into the early-morning hours. Their conversations shifted to a myriad of topics until enjoyment finally gave way to exhaustion. "Come on, it's getting late. I'll show you to your cabin."

Chapter 7

David took a cold shower that lasted twenty minutes and still he tossed and turned most of the night. Having Natalia sleeping in the cabin right next to him set his nerves on fire, but he suppressed his desires. It was more than the physical. She had gotten to him. The emptiness he'd always felt inside and hidden so well had begun to fill. But he knew that last night wasn't the right time for them to be together. One sleepless night didn't bother him—much.

At daybreak, the vibrant sky came alive and the tranquility of contentment surrounded him as they woke up in the Bahamas. He sat out on the deck sipping mango juice and waiting for Natalia to try on some of the clothes he had delivered to her cabin earlier. Staring out at the horizon, he began to feel guilty. He knew he was doing this for the right reason. He just wasn't sure now that it was the right way. Maybe Pam was right.

Maybe he should have just come out and told her the truth from the beginning. But how do you tell a woman that you're the biological father of her two sons?

He smiled, remembering the photos from last night. The two boys were handsome, just as he'd expected. They also kept him up all night thinking. He was going about this all wrong and this role he was playing was getting too complicated. To top it off, he was way past getting emotionally attached. His heart was starting to yield.

Her grace and tranquil personality were magnetic. Her heart was giving and her spirit was caring and open. She was everything he'd always wanted. He genuinely enjoyed being with her.

"Good morning."

David turned, seeing Natalia standing in the doorway dressed in a flowing floral-patterned sundress. A gentle breeze blew around her body, accenting the sweet curve of her hips and her slender frame. "Good morning. Wow, look at you." He paused and shook his head. "You look fantastic in that outfit." She pivoted slightly to show the halter-style dress and billowing bow at the back of her neck.

"Thank you," she said, nodding graciously. "And thank you for the clothes. They're beautiful. But you really bought too many. We're only gonna be here one day. There are five outfits in my cabin."

"I guess it's a leftover impulse from my sister. She always said that women can never have too many clothes. How'd you sleep?"

"After a late-night brandy, three glasses of champagne and the motion of the ocean, I slept like a baby," Natalia confessed. "I can see why you travel by water. It's so soothing."

"Actually, I travel by water for relaxation and privacy. Very few paparazzi can tread water for hours at a time or are fortunate enough to own a speedboat."

"So that's your secret."

"Secret?"

"I looked you up on the Internet the other day. There are a lot of photos of you early on in your career, but not a lot now."

"You mean photos with women?" he asked.

She nodded. "Now it's like you dropped off the paparazzi radar or something."

"I wish. They're still out there, but I've just made it a little harder for them to get to me."

"So in other words you can basically do whatever you want now without having photos of yourself plastered all over the magazines and tabloid covers."

"Or on the Internet," he added.

"Smart."

"It doesn't always work."

"Looks like it did this time," she said, walking over to the rail while looking around at the vast horizon and dazzling beauty around her. The vibrant colors were breathtaking—lush, verdant greenery and brilliant floral displays were everywhere. "Wow, it's so beautiful here, so peaceful and quiet." She turned suddenly and looked down the length of the dock. "There's no one around. Where are we exactly?"

"We're in the Bahamas—South Bimini, to be exact. It's one of my favorite places."

"Bimini. I've always wanted to come here. It's so lovely," she whispered, looking around in wonder.

"Yes, you are," he said, staring at her in the morning light. She was a vision. The colorful dress accented her slim waist and the smooth sloping sway of her back and derriere. He couldn't resist touching her. "I thought we'd grab some breakfast on board then have a look around town. There's some really fascinating architecture and I think you're gonna love the shops here."

"Sounds perfect," she said, following him to the table set out on the deck just as breakfast was being served. They ate quickly then started their day. Walking down the dock, they passed a small cottage up on a hill. "Doesn't this dock belong to the people who live in the cottage up there?"

"Yes."

"So you know them," she affirmed.

"It belongs to a good friend of mine."

She nodded and continued walking as she wondered who the "good friend" might be. She'd seen him with so many different women in the Internet photos that it had left an impression. Models, movie stars, heiresses, entertainers—they were all beautiful, poised and famous. She'd often read magazine headlines coupling David with other movie stars, particularly his leading ladies. There was one that even had him breaking up a married couple, but that proved to be just tabloid fodder. "A friend as in one from those Internet photos?" she asked.

He chuckled softly, knowing what she was thinking. "No, sorry to disappoint you," he said. "My good friend is a musician who comes here to write music when he's not touring. He grew up in a small community not too far from here called Port Royale."

Natalia nodded, happy that he'd elaborated. They continued walking past exquisite homes with scenery that was breathtaking. Talking and walking, the next two hours seemed like only ten minutes. Just before midday they stopped and sat at a small outdoor café for a snack and a quick drink. "This place is so incredible," Natalia said, feeling the slow, relaxing island rhythm all around her. "It's hard to believe that people actually live here all the time. I'd never get anything done."

He stood and took her hand to help her up. They walked through town hand in hand, stopping occasionally for an autograph or to window-shop. "I can't believe you've never been here before."

"Traveling is my sister's thing, not mine. Tatiana has been to every continent, either as a correspondent or just for the joy of traveling."

"What about your other sister, Nikita?"

"She lived in London and Paris for a time."

"But you've always stayed in the Keys."

She nodded. "Pretty much. I'm basically a homebody."

They continued talking as they walked through the narrow promenades and stopped at several street vendors. They laughed and talked, enjoying each moment they spent together. "Oh, look at this. Brice would look so cute in it," Natalia said, smiling at a tiny colorful shirt in the front window. "I have to get this for him."

"Allow me," David said.

"No, really, you've done enough already. I'll be right back."

David watched as she walked into the small shop and picked up a miniature floral shirt and held it up. She smiled and then began looking for others. She collected another shirt and two T-shirts, one for each child, then turned to show him. He smiled and nodded his approval. She looked around a bit more, then, finding one other item, she paid and left the shop.

She found David instantly. He was standing with three starry-eyed women. They talked, laughed and giggled incessantly as they took turns taking photos with him. The last to have her photo taken made sure to press her ample breasts into his side. Before the photo was taken, he glanced over to the shop's entrance and smiled. The buxom woman quickly turned to see who had gotten his attention. Natalia smiled and nodded to David, picking up the one woman's annoyed reaction out of the corner of her eye. She walked to the next shop and looked at the display. The last thing she needed was to hit the cover of a tabloid. David walked over a few minutes later and suggested that they head back to the dock. She readily agreed.

By noon, they were back on the boat in bathing suits, preparing to go snorkeling. It was the perfect day, as turquoise water sparkled beneath the midday sun. They dove into the water, skimming the surface and enjoying the beauty along the coral reefs below. Later, they walked along the private white sand beach as the foam water crests danced at their feet and lazy palm trees swayed in the warm breeze.

"So tell me about acting. Is that what you always wanted to do when you were growing up?"

"No, not really. I never really thought about it until later. I did some modeling and commercials to pay for college and then I just sort of transitioned into acting."

"Are you working now?"

"Actually, I just finished shooting a movie."

"What's it called?" she asked curiously.

"Its working title is *Cross My Heart,*" he said, then began to tell her about the basic premise of a man finding an unlikely love after surviving an illness. She asked more questions as they turned and headed back to the boat. By the time they arrived, Natalia couldn't wait to see the movie.

"It sounds very different from your usual work. What made you decide to do it?"

"You're right. It is very different. But it's a great script and the casting, directing and cinematography are brilliant. I think it's going to be very well received."

When they got back to the boat, Natalia excused herself to call Mia and check on the boys. Mia told her that Stephen and her brothers had taken Brice fishing. Her father and grandfather tagged along to round out the party. She expected them back later. "Are you enjoying yourself?" Mia asked.

"Yes, way too much," Natalia answered. "I'm in Bimini and it's like paradise here. We went into town for a while, then did some snorkeling and afterwards just strolled along a private sand beach. David is really great to be with."

"Sounds like you're finally taking a minute for yourself."

"I am, and I don't feel nearly as guilty about it as I thought I would."

"Guilty? Why on earth should you feel guilty?" she asked.

"I'm a mom. My children are my first responsibility."

"Yes, you're a mom, but you're a woman, too. Where does it say that motherhood precludes you from having a life?"

"It's just that I see families all the time with parents who just seem to give up and walk away. I never want to be like that."

"You won't. You can't. You're not wired like that. Just because you take one weekend to enjoy yourself doesn't make you a terrible person. It makes you human. So enjoy your movie star and come back relaxed, stress free and with tons of juicy gossip to share. Deal?"

Natalia chuckled.

"Great, now get back to that gorgeous man and get wild."

"You know what? I think I just might." Natalia giggled.

"Now that's what I'm talking 'bout. See ya later. Enjoy."

After Mia hung up, Natalia went back out onto the deck, where David was pouring a tall flute of champagne. "Perfect timing. We're just about to get under way."

"We're heading back?" she asked, trying not to sound as disappointed as she was.

"No, I thought we'd do something special for dinner this evening."

She looked at him curiously. "Special? How special?"

"My surprise."

Chapter 8

Miami nightlife was hot, sultry, sexy and definitely not to be believed. By the time the boat landed, they'd changed clothes and were ready to go. David looked every inch the coolly immaculate movie star, complete with hat and dark sunglasses. Natalia was admittedly stunning in a thin-strapped, floral-silk wrap minidress, trimmed in hot pink with matching stiletto sandals. David intended to show her a night in his world.

They ate dinner at a huge glitzy restaurant, receiving first-class service and attention. Lobsters, steaks and seafood covered their table as champagne and drinks flowed like water. Later they club-hopped, dancing reggae to steel drums, salsa and calypso with maracas and freestyle with the latest hip-hop artists. They hit three clubs with music as unique and varied as the people themselves.

By the time they got back to the yacht, they were

exhausted yet still energized. They stayed on deck talking and enjoying their last few hours together. The engine hummed as they prepared to head back to Key West. Natalia leaned back against the rail as music played softly all around them. Smiling incessantly, she looked up at the millions of stars sparkling like diamonds above her head and then sighed. "My head is still spinning. I think I had way too much fun tonight."

"No way. You can never have too much fun," David said.

"Maybe you can't, but I live in the real world where this doesn't happen every weekend. In fact, this never happens."

"I'm glad you had a good time."

Natalia chuckled, remembering the day's events. "Correction. I had an *amazing* time. As a matter of fact, I had an amazing time all weekend."

"I'm glad," he said sincerely.

"The past few days have been absolutely magical. Thank you. You have no idea how much I needed this getaway," she said.

"Actually, *you* made it magical for me."

"I still can't believe I spent Saturday in Bimini and tonight in Miami."

"Why not? It's just a matter of deciding to do it."

"For you, maybe. But I don't do impulsive."

"Sometimes impulsive can be simply wonderful."

She shook her head slowly. "No, impulsive can get you in trouble. Impulsive can lower your defenses and entice you without your even knowing it."

Without hesitation he leaned in. His lips touched hers leisurely and long, lingering so slowly it seemed as if time itself had slowed for them. She closed her eyes, reveling in the feel of his mouth, then wrapped her arms around his neck as she opened to him. His tongue slipped inside, then delved deep into her, tasting the sweet essence of her desire. How could a kiss be this mind-blowing and still so sweet? He turned, reversing course, leaning his back against the rail and pulling her against his body. She moved closer, pressing against him until she felt his penis harden. She knew it was for her. The knowledge ignited the already churning, burning fire in her stomach, setting in motion a raging inferno.

Her thoughts spun, her legs weakened and her body went limp. She yielded and lay against him, his one hand spread wide on her back, his other hand holding the nape of her neck to deepen the kiss. They swam, locked in unimaginable bliss, kissing, caressing, touching and feeling the intense desire surging within and between them. Then the kiss slowly ended. Breathless, she rolled her head and arched back. He burned a trail of kisses down her neck, over her shoulders then back up to her lips again. His hands caressed her, stroking the softness between their molded bodies.

"That was impulsive and that was nice," he said.

"Yes, it was. But that was also trouble," she added.

"I've wanted to do that all night," he muttered, kissing her tenderly then nuzzling her neck and holding her close as he stroked the roundness of her breasts and her nipples instantly hardened for him. She gasped, feeling the sensation press against the silky material. He teased her and she yielded and responded. "David." It had been too long. "David." He groaned, enjoying the sound of his name on her lips until he silenced her with another kiss. She was on fire and every nerve in her body was ready to explode. She didn't just want him. No, she needed him. She needed him now.

A few seconds later, the kiss ended. They were both breathless and off balance. She laid her head against his chest, praying that this dizzying feeling would never end. The thunderous pounding of his heart and the stiff hardness pressing against her was telling. He wanted her, too. He held her tight as he caressed and stroked her back lovingly.

They stood silent, each debating the right and wrong of the moment. This was where reason returned and emotion receded. Natalia closed her eyes and took a deep breath, feeling the protective embrace of a man she knew would sooner or later break her heart. But her emotions were all over the place. This was all happening too fast. Still, the clarity of her desire could not be denied. "What am I doing here with you?" she whispered more to herself than to him.

"This doesn't have to go any further. A kiss is just a kiss."

"I think we both know better than that," she whispered.

She was right. David closed his eyes and kissed her forehead. In just a few weeks she had changed his life and now, in just a few moments, she had devastated his entire body. He was on fire. No woman had ever affected him as she did. He tipped her chin and looked into her wanton eyes, knowing that she felt that exact same fire and that he wanted her now more than ever, but not this way. She needed to know everything.

Natalia leaned up to kiss him. He leaned back and away. But she wasn't having it. "Don't tell me you're gonna be shy," she said as she started unbuttoning his shirt, then kissed his neck.

David closed his eyes, feeling her lips on his neck and chest. His body was already hard, but to his amazement she was getting him even more excited. The thing was that he knew he needed to tell her about their connection. "Natalia, wait," he held her hands. "There's something I need to tell you."

"Don't you think we've talked enough the past few days?" she asked as she reached up to kiss him again. This time she nuzzled his neck and chest.

He closed his eyes and groaned. "No, wait, you need to know about me, about us, about why I'm here."

"I don't care why you're here. I'm just glad you are." She wanted him and she knew that he wanted her. The waiting and wanting was consuming her. She placed her hands around his neck and drew him in. She kissed him. Passion and longing ruled. He held her as the kiss deepened. Their tongues intertwined in possessive passion.

When the kiss ended, he stepped back and walked away. "Natalia." He took a deep, cleansing breath to recite the most difficult monologue of his life.

"Don't," she whispered, moving to stand behind him. "Don't. We've been dancing around this all evening; for days, in fact. I know it and I know you know it. There's an attraction—we both feel it, we both know it," she said. "I know what I want, David. I want you. Do you want me?"

He turned. His voice caught in his throat. The mere

KIMANI™
ROMANCE

An Important Message from the Publisher

Dear Reader,

Because you've chosen to read one of our fine novels, I'd like to say "thank you"! And, as a special way to say thank you, I'm offering to send you two more Kimani™ Romance novels and two surprise gifts – absolutely FREE! These books will keep it real with true-to-life African American characters that turn up the heat and sizzle with passion.

Please enjoy the free books and gifts with our compliments...

Glenda Howard

For Kimani Press

Peel off Seal and Place Inside...

FREE GIFTS
EDITOR'S SEAL
THANK YOU

THE EDITOR'S "THANK YOU" FREE GIFTS INCLUDE:

▶ Two Kimani™ Romance Novels
▶ Two exciting surprise gifts

YES! I have placed my
Editor's "thank you" Free Gifts
seal in the space provided at
right. Please send me 2 FREE
books, and my 2 FREE
Mystery Gifts. I understand
that I am under no obligation
to purchase anything further, as
explained on the back of this card.

PLACE
FREE GIFTS
SEAL
HERE

About how many NEW paperback fiction books have you purchased
in the past 3 months?

❏ 0-2   ❏ 3-6   ❏ 7 or more
EZQE   EZQQ   EZQ2

168/368 XDL

FIRST NAME

LAST NAME

ADDRESS

APT.#

CITY

STATE/PROV.

ZIP/POSTAL CODE

Thank You!

If offer card is missing write to: The Reader Service, P.O. Box 1867, Buffalo, NY 14240-1867 or visit us at www.ReaderService.com

BUSINESS REPLY MAIL

FIRST-CLASS MAIL   PERMIT NO. 717   BUFFALO, NY

POSTAGE WILL BE PAID BY ADDRESSEE

THE READER SERVICE
PO BOX 1867
BUFFALO NY 14240-9952

NO POSTAGE
NECESSARY
IF MAILED
IN THE
UNITED STATES

questioning of his desire for her was ludicrous. He wanted her more than anything. "Yes, yes, you know I want you, too. But this may not be what we need to do right now. I don't know where this is going and I don't want to lie to you." She looked up at him as he stared down at her. "I can't promise you happily ever after," he said. She smiled. He took her hand and kissed it. "Natalia," he said, touching the side of her face.

She'd always been clear on what she wanted out of life—a career, a family and love. She'd found a career she enjoyed and had a family she cherished, loved and adored. But love had always been elusive. She had never found her Mr. Right. So when it came to David, she was very clear. Tonight was for her. Now it didn't matter how long it would last.

Instinctively, she wouldn't open her heart because hearts got broken. She'd seen it a hundred times in her job. No, this was physical. This was sex. She wanted his body—hard, firm and solid. "I don't want happily ever after. I just want tonight. I want right now. Make love to me, David."

"I want nothing more than to make love to you right now, Natalia, but I don't want you to regret this later."

"Regrets are for those who want and expect more. I don't. I know what I want. I know what this is." She took his hand. "Take me to your cabin."

Chapter 9

Take me to your cabin.

Her simple request set his body on fire all over again. He swept her into his arms and kissed her. Passion erupted as she molded her body to his, giving them each what they craved. The fantasy of being in his arms was real and that reality was larger than any fantasy she could possibly imagine. The kiss deepened and they were consumed by the overwhelming feelings growing inside. Blinding passion covered them as the kiss enveloped the moment. Her knees weakened as his arms circled her waist and she wrapped her arms around his neck.

"I never knew how hungry I was until I met you," he whispered as the kiss ended and everything else began. He licked and nibbled and tasted her, relishing her neck and shoulders as his hands drifted to her breasts. He felt each nipple harden in the palm of his hand. Now just feeling the rounded orbs wasn't enough. He wanted more. He wanted all of her. His body shook and tensed as his penis throbbed with need.

She gasped, holding her breath and nearly exploding inside. A split second of nervousness needled through her. She hadn't done this in a while and never with a man she'd only known for a few days. But somehow the length of time didn't matter. In her heart she felt as if she'd known him all her life. She closed her eyes, letting the thick haze of desire surrounding them consume her. When she opened her eyes, he was smiling at her. It was all the reassurance she needed. She looked deep into his penetrating eyes.

"Are you okay?" he asked softly. She nodded. "I want you so badly."

"Then show me," she said breathlessly. "Show me."

He led her back into the salon, then they descended the glass- and wood-framed circular staircase. They walked down a narrow corridor to arched double doors at the end of the hall. He opened both doors and she walked in first. There was a stylish sitting area with a desk, bookcase, sofa and chairs, just like in the upstairs salon. She walked into the room, following the natural path of the décor. As soon as she turned the far corner, she saw a huge, plush bed in the middle of the room.

Raised up on red mahogany panels, it was loaded down with pillows and a gold paisley duvet that looked like it had been stuffed with clouds. The lighting in the room was subdued and the same soft, melodious music that played in the salon upstairs played down here, as well. "Wow, this is so beautiful." She walked into the room farther and looked around. Wherever she turned she was amazed at the exquisite beauty. She stopped at the large bed against the far wall. After running her hand over the top, she sat then lay back, looking over at him. He'd stayed back, leaning against the wall's built-in cabinetry, watching her. "Are you going to join me?"

He smiled easily as he walked over and stood beside the bed. "Actually, I'm enjoying the view. You are the epitome of perfection lying there," he said, his voice still husky with desire.

"Is that right?" she said as she bit her lower lip seductively while sitting up on her knees, and reached out to touch him as he approached. "Do you want to touch me?" she teased. He nodded. "Well, you're gonna have to wait your turn."

Teasing wasn't her style, but right here, right now it felt so right. She wanted this to be unforgettable and she intended to try anything and everything she ever imagined and fantasized. She placed her hand on his chest. His heart was beating rapidly. She reached up and caressed his face then boldly began unbuttoning the rest of his shirt. When she finished, she pushed it back over his shoulders and then tossed it onto the chair closest to the bed. Smiling at the full sight of him, she gently raked her nails down his neck, his shoulders, his chest and then down to his tightly muscled stomach. She felt him quiver and shudder, so she gave her intrepid spirit free rein. The smooth, hot feel of his body enticed her to become bolder in her actions.

She leaned in and blew on his tiny pebbled nipple like a birthday candle. His body jerked in response. She stopped and looked up into his eyes. Seeing that his desire had grown tenfold, she went back to his nipple and blew again. He jerked again. She licked him, she kissed him, she nibbled him. Each time she felt his body tense and his muscles tighten. The sensation of having this control over him was intoxicating. "I think you like that," she said as she leaned up and whispered into his ear, then licked his lobe. "Do you like that?" she asked; her hot breath tantalizing his ear made his body quake again. He nodded slowly. "Do you want me to stop?" He shook his head no. Happily, she continued. Then, moments later, she decided that teasing and touching him wasn't enough. It was time to step up her game.

She unbuckled his belt and pulled it free from the loops. Then she unhooked and unzipped his pants and let them fall to the carpet. He let her take charge as the muscle in his jaw visibly tightened. She looked down, admiring the hefty bulge in his boxer briefs. Her task wasn't quite complete; still, she smiled and nodded her success. Anticipation propelled her to move from the bed and stand in front of him. With her hands sure and skillful, she eased around the elastic waistband, then started pulling them down. But her private enjoyment didn't last for long. He grabbed her wrists, smiled and shook his head.

"My turn now," he said thickly as he sat on the bed and pulled her waist toward him, reversing their positions. Spoken plainly, they were words of warning, words of promise. Of course he wasn't going to make it that easy for her. She looked into his eyes. Half-hooded, they had a gleam that she'd never seen before. Placed intently between his legs, she stood waiting for whatever he had in mind. He looked her up and down then grabbed the soft fabric belt tied around her waist and pulled the bow free. The dress instantly opened. He stared at her exposed body with delightful pleasure. He knew she'd had two children, but to look at her body, no one could ever tell.

Full and luscious, her ample breasts were covered by a thin lace bra. Her stomach was completely flat and her legs were long and shapely. He pushed the dress back over her shoulders and let it slowly fall to the floor. He reached out and touched her breasts then ran his hand down the front of her body, stopping when he got to the lace panties. She gasped. He turned her around slowly. The back of her was just as enticing.

Touching her, he reached up across her shoulders then eased down her back until he got to the elastic waistband again. Her rounded cheeks were perfect, just the right size and shape. Grasping one, then the other, he pulled her back, pressing his face to her lower back as he continued to stroke and massage her rear. He kissed her, then wrapped his hands around front and held her breasts in the palms of his hands as he licked and tantalized her back. His rhythm was easy and fluid. Breathless, her legs weakened. She leaned back, almost staggering. He held her in place, continuing to kiss and nibble her body. She arched her back and looked down, seeing his hands on her breasts and feeling his mouth now biting and nibbling her derriere. The feeling was intense and she was wet all over again. "David, let's do this," she muttered.

"Umm, not yet, my darling. I have so much more to touch."

True to his word, he touched her, caressed her and fondled her. Her mind shattered. His hands were masterful and she knew she couldn't take much more. She was almost ready to explode. "I want you inside me now," she whispered.

"Soon," he promised. "Soon."

She writhed against him as he continued his assault. His hands all over her body, his mouth kissing, licking and nipping everywhere—it was maddening. He leaned her up to steady her on her feet, then turned her around. The sight of her lace-covered breasts hit him instantly. With one flick of the front closure, he freed her. The full heaviness of her perfectly formed orbs and the delicate nipples sent him over the top. He grabbed her and pulled her forward. She arched her back as his mouth opened and he took one nipple and breast into his mouth. He suckled, licked, teased it, and she shook from the excitement. She grasped his shoulders to halt him, but he was too intent. He backed off and took the other nipple and breast into his mouth. She closed her eyes and moaned. He felt so good. Her panting breathing increased.

Now, both breasts pressed together, he took his time and indulged his hunger. Still holding on to his shoulders, she barely managed to steady herself. She placed her knee on the bed, then moved to straddle his body as he sat. The position found her sitting on his lap, his covered penis pressed firmly against her covered core. He continued licking and suckling her and she began gyrating her body to the slow rhythm she felt inside. Slowly, he kissed her breasts, then her chest, her neck and finally he found her mouth.

The kiss exploded, from abandoned hunger to unrestrained rapture. He ravaged her mouth with an unyielding hold so strong she thought that her body would literally disintegrate. Still she held tight, needing everything he gave. There was no beginning and no ending. Her body was etched into his. She moaned, he groaned and the guttural mix of their voices seemed to intensify their passion. They were ablaze.

Her heart never pumped so fast or so hard. Her body quivered. The sensual turbulence was mind-boggling. The kiss broke without warning. They looked into each other's eyes. Both exhausted and breathless, they knew this was only the start of their pleasure. She stood and stepped back. He looked at her, questioning. She took a deep breath. "We need some…"

"…got 'em." He nodded, stood, opening the side table and pulling out a box of condoms. He pulled one out and placed the box on the table. He removed his boxer briefs. His penis was thick, long, hard and ready for her. He opened the small packet and watched as she took it from him, then looked up as she pulled it out. She unrolled it a bit then eased it onto the tip of his penis. She saw his stomach tighten and lurch. When she was done she moved farther back onto the bed and lay back.

He came to her, hovering and looking down at this perfect woman. She was exquisite in every way—her body, her mind and her spirit. This was going to happen and he wanted it to be the most unforgettable experience for her. He knew right then that once with her would never be enough. She grasped the elastic waistband on her panties, but he stopped her. "Not yet, close your eyes," he instructed softly.

She nodded and complied, closing her eyes and waiting. He moved her hands above her head, then she felt his mouth on her body again, starting on her shoulders, kissing and licking down to her toes, then back up. When he got to her panties, he encircled the band, then slowly eased them down. Tiny silky hairs barely covered the treasure he sought. He spread her legs, placing one over his shoulder, then he lowered his head and blew. Seconds later he touched the tiny nub, stroking her needful wetness. She gasped, her legs shook and she writhed, knowing his intent.

She arched her back off the bed. He leaned up. His mouth covered her breasts and his fingers entered her. She was tight, yet the intense pleasure she felt was pure rapture as he continued to probe and stretch her body to fit his. "Now, David, now." The dam of restraint was shattering, but he continued to stretch her body. Then he moved above her, and entered halfway in one smooth motion. She shrieked, nearly screaming. Her body tensed. She felt as if she were on fire. She held her breath and dug her nails into his shoulders.

David froze, struggling to retain the last remnant of restraint. She was tight, far tighter than he expected. "Did I hurt you?" he rasped with effort. She didn't reply. Her eyes were closed and he could see that she held her breath. "Natalia, breathe. Listen to me. Look at me." She opened her eyes. "Are you in pain?"

She smiled. "It'll pass." Before she got the last word out she arched her hips upward, forcing her body to wholly engulf him. The exquisite pain of being completely filled by him was intense. She began rocking her hips, rubbing against him. He moved with her, slowly at first, then they increased the rhythm.

They thrust with fierce intensity, each stroke

increased in speed and depth. In and out, they met power for power. Surging stronger, the swell of pleasure overtook her. She came and tensed, panting the rapture of her climax.

Seconds later she realized that he was still hard inside her. This time his movements were slow and purposeful. Weak and drained, she lay there as he toyed with her body, drawing a second, third and fourth climax. Then he moved faster, joining their bodies again and again, pushing in and pulling out, seeming to test the limits of her sanity. Finding her strength, she pounded up into him. Faster, fuller, in simultaneous consumption, they came together. Their bodies went stiff as each spasm took them and his body drained every ounce of essence into her.

Moments later he rolled over, lay back on the bed and looked up at the ceiling. He closed his eyes, feeling the last remnants of their lovemaking still with him. Being inside of her was wonderful, being with her tonight was breathtaking. She was everything he wanted in a woman and the fact that she already had his sons only increased his feelings. He opened his eyes and looked over to Natalia. She hadn't moved. He reached over and gathered her in his embrace. He needed her close.

Natalia moaned and sighed as her skin prickled. Her body was still reeling from their lovemaking. He pulled her close and she complied willingly; being wrapped in his arms felt utterly right. The only problem was that she knew it wouldn't last. Fantasies never did. Still, she closed her eyes and held on tight. She didn't know what kind of ride she was in for. But she intended to enjoy it for as long as it lasted.

"You okay over there?" he asked softly, beginning to stroke her back gently.

"Absolutely, blissfully wonderful," she replied.

"I like the sound of that."

She sighed again. "I don't know how I'm gonna wrap my head around the real world after this," she murmured to herself.

"What do you mean?" he asked.

"I mean that I know this isn't real," she said as she rolled up to sit beside him. She looked down into his eyes. "You aren't real and I need to always keep that in mind."

He sat up and kissed her tenderly. "I'm very real, Natalia. And this—you and I here, right now—is as real as it gets."

"For you, yes, but not for me. I'm a down-to-earth person, David. This is a dream, and pretty soon I'm going to have to wake up, whether I want to or not. I can't allow myself the luxury of..." She paused.

"...feeling anything for me?" he asked. "Or falling in love with me?"

"Either. Both."

They were silent, just looking into each other's eyes. He picked up her hand and kissed it. "Natalia, I don't know what's going to happen tomorrow or the next day or the day after that. I do know that I want to be in your life for as long as you'll have me. Is that okay?"

She nodded. "Yeah, that's okay."

"Good. Now how about something to nibble on."

"You, sir, are spoiling me," she moaned.

"And this is only the beginning. What would you like?"

"You," she said seductively.

"Sounds good to me. Your wish is my command." He held her tight as they kissed. This time the kiss was long and lazy as they savored the pleasure they'd just experienced. He reached for and grabbed another condom. She smiled, nodding slowly. She had a few more wishes for him to grant.

Chapter 10

Being on the phone while walking quickly through a hotel lobby is a classic Hollywood celebrity trick to ensure minimal public interruption. Few fans would make a spectacle of themselves by running after and disturbing a seemingly preoccupied celebrity for a photo or autograph. But this morning David didn't do it out of the necessity for privacy. He did it because of Natalia. He'd just dropped her off at her home and already he was feeling the pangs of wanting to be with her again.

"You were stunning this morning," he said quietly as he quickly strolled into the hotel and headed to the private elevator near the front desk.

"Where are you?" Natalia asked.

"Walking through the hotel lobby headed toward the private elevator. Why? Feel like a little phone sex this morning?" he joked.

Natalia laughed. "You're incorrigible. Thanks,

but no thanks. I'm sitting in my home office doing the paperwork I was supposed to complete Friday evening."

"Regrets?"

"Hardly. I had a wonderful time. You know I had a wonderful time. I still can't believe the past two days," Natalia said.

"Which part?"

"How about all of it?" she said, chuckling softly. "But I'd have to admit that waking up Saturday morning docked in the Bahamas was definitely the topper."

"I'm glad you weren't upset about my little detour."

"Upset, no. A bit stunned, definitely. It was quite a surprise to wake up hearing steel drums playing in the background."

"I'm glad you enjoyed yourself."

"I did. Thank you. Now as for the clothes you bought me…"

"We're not going over that again, are we?"

"We are, because I intend to pay you back."

"The trip was impromptu. Understandably, you weren't prepared. I had my staff pick a few things up when we arrived in port. You were still asleep. Problem solved. The idea of having you naked and in bed with me all day was definitely tempting, but I eventually decided to share you with the rest of the world."

"A *few things* would constitute a sundress, panties and flip-flops, not five complete outfits, including bathing suits, a straw hat and a thong."

"Okay, granted, the thong was definitely my idea and I do most sincerely appreciate you trying it on for me," he said, grinning at the memory of her standing in the cabin's dressing-room doorway with just the thong and stilettos on. His body hardened instantly—then and now. Her breasts were firm and round and her nipples were hard as diamonds. Her narrow waist was trim and slid graciously into the scant piece of elastic lace. It was white—purity came to mind. But seeing her standing there, purity had nothing to do with what he wanted to do to her body.

"I'd never worn one before," she said, laughing.

"Well let me be the first and only one to say that you wear it very, very well." He stopped just short of requesting that she wear a thong for no one else but him from now on. "As a matter of fact, I think I'm going to have to pick up a few more for you, not that you had that one on for very long."

She laughed again at the image of him dashing across the cabin to get to her. "True. It took me longer to put it on than for you to take it off. I'm still surprised at how fast you moved."

"Desire is a great motivator and to get to you in just a thong…" He paused, closed his eyes, bowed his head and leaned back against the elevator wall. The image of her standing there, posed, arms over her head, legs spread apart hit him again. "I would have moved heaven and earth…" He licked his lips, tasting the last of her kiss on his mouth. He shuddered. He wanted her all over again. "Then when you turned around with your back to me…" He paused again, taking a slow deep breath. But it didn't help.

The memory was crystal clear. As soon as he got to her, he'd dropped down on his knees with his face at two perfectly rounded cheeks. He rubbed his hands over her behind, down her thighs, then between her legs and up to her hardened nipples and breasts. Her knees buckled as he pulled at and removed the thong. She stepped out of it and he grabbed her leg to put over his shoulder. With her arms still braced above her head, she held tight to the door frame as he feasted, kissing, sucking, nibbling frantically. She came almost instantly. Afterwards, they made love on the carpet right there in the doorway. It was fast and furious. He barely had time to grab a condom and put it on. He'd never experienced such mind-blowing, explosive intensity before. His body shuddered repeatedly. Even now, with the erotic memory irrevocably and firmly in place, he tensed. "You know, I was joking before about the phone sex, but to tell you the truth…"

"Sorry, babe. We're off Fantasy Island. It's back to reality now," she said sadly.

"Woman, you're killing me over here," he whispered huskily.

"Not my intention, I assure you. But if it makes you feel any better, man, you're killing me over here, too." Her voice dropped down an octave and slowed seductively.

"It does, but not much. I want you so bad right now."

"I know. Me, too. But you know that we can't get too carried away with this. *I* can't get too carried away," she clarified. "I can't just think about myself."

"I know, and that makes you even more desirable." He took a deep breath, then exhaled slowly. "Okay, we either need to change the subject or you'd better pull out that thong, 'cause I'm hungry and I'm headed back to your house."

"The last thing I want to be responsible for is you getting a speeding ticket trying to get over here, so I guess we'd better change the subject," she said. "So what's on your schedule today?"

"Nothing that can't wait. Why? What do you have in mind?"

"I thought we were changing the subject."

"You're right. So have you spoken to your sons yet?" he asked, hoping to defuse his need for her. It didn't work. He suspected nothing ever would.

"No, not this morning. They were still asleep when I called a few minutes ago. Mia's going to call me back as soon as they wake up. It's so odd," she said, looking around. "The house is so quiet and empty without them here with me. I forgot what it was like living alone."

David considered for an instant what his house would be like with the joyous noise of his children around. It would probably drive him crazy, he assured himself. He was too used to peace and quiet and the sanity of life on his own. There was no way he could tolerate having his world disrupted with the job and responsibility of parenthood. Still, there was a small nagging voice that questioned the thought. "I was sitting here trying to remember what I did before I had them," she continued. "I can't even remember what life was like before. I do know that it was empty."

"Why did you do it?" he asked plainly, unexpectedly.

"Do what? Have Brice and Jayden?"

"Yeah," he said, realizing that the question hung over

everything between them. It was the reason why he was there and it was the reason why he was feeling what he was feeling all of a sudden.

"It's hard to explain because there are so many reasons. I wanted to bring life into the world. I wanted to take care of someone. But I guess the main reason is that I have a lot of love to give and because I wanted—no, I needed—to have a child. With Brice and Jayden, love is unconditional. There is nothing I wouldn't do to make them happy."

"Why not get married first and have children? Why go to a sperm bank?" She went silent. "You there?" he asked.

"Yes. You do ask tough questions, don't you?"

"It was intrusive. You don't have to answer," he said.

"No, I want to. Finding a man and getting married isn't as easy as it sounds. I dated, of course. I was even engaged before, but it wasn't love; it was familiarity. It was expected. It was a mistake. Ultimately, I didn't want to bring my child into a relationship that wasn't complete. Finding a man is easy. Finding love is the hard part. There was no guarantee on how long finding love would take or if in fact I ever would, so I decided to have children on my own."

"It sounds a lot like you've completely given up on love."

"No, I wouldn't say that I've completely given up on love and I would rather not resign myself to a life alone. I think I'm just very selective now. I have my sons to consider. Every decision I made affects their happiness, too."

"Then I guess I should be honored that you even agreed to go to dinner with me, let alone spend the weekend with me."

"If I seem overly cautious when I'm out with you, it's because I've gotten my heart broken a few times and you are just way too dangerous."

"Dangerous? What do you mean? Are you talking about the fans and the paparazzi?"

"No. Thankfully, I'm not significant enough for anyone to notice me. When we were out at the clubs in Miami, all eyes were on you. The women, the men—they adore you. I was just happy to step back and enjoy the spectacle."

"You're right. It's all a spectacle, a fantasy. They don't really know me. So it's not the press or the fans. So what's the dangerous part about me?"

"It's you. You're dangerous. You're the perfect guy—alpha male, the quintessential hero. Television, stage, movies, fame—you're who women fantasize about. You're a superhero, literally, if what I hear rumored on the entertainment channel is correct."

"Yes, I've been cast in that role, but it's all a mask, a part I play. I'm not really that guy. I hope you know that by now."

"Yes, of course I do. But it doesn't change the fact that you're still dangerous to the heart—to my heart."

He didn't agree, but he understood what she meant. "So are you still looking for Mr. Right?"

"I'm not looking for Mr. Right. I'm looking for Mr. Love Me for Me—as I am."

"I see," he said, considering her reply.

"What about you? Marriage, children—are you looking for Ms. Right?" she asked.

"Possibly."

"That's surprising."

"Why surprising?" he asked.

"I guess I never expected that you'd be looking for the 'Happily Ever After' thing. You seem more like the 'bachelor for life' type."

"If you'd asked me a few months ago, I would have said no. My life was perfect at that point. I was happy, my career was steady and my biggest dilemma was which script to read first. Now so many things have changed."

"Either way, it must be really hard for you."

"What do you mean?" he asked.

"Finding someone when you're so famous. How do you know if the woman you're interested in is drawn to you for your money and what you have? Or for who you are or what you can do for her career? You're a movie star. I imagine you must be bombarded with propositions."

"It's not as difficult as you would think. There are the obvious gold diggers, of course, and then the more subtle ones, but ultimately they all make a very telling mistake. After you've been in the business a while, you learn to see through them instantly and weed them out automatically."

"And the ones you don't see through instantly?" she asked.

"You make mistakes and get your heart broken, just like everybody else."

"Well, just to set your mind at ease, I don't care

about the money and fame. I'm only with you for your body."

He chuckled. "I like that answer," he said happily. "So what are your plans today?" he asked, changing the subject again.

"Well, after I finish this paperwork, I'll be hanging out in your neck of the woods. Niki and I have an appointment at the day spa in the hotel."

"Sounds like fun," he said.

"It will be. We always have a great time together and when my other sister, Tatiana, is in town we have a blast. So, yeah, I'm looking forward to it," she said.

"Natalia, Nikita and Tatiana—interesting names," he remarked.

"I have four siblings all together. Dominik and Mikhail are my brothers and as I'm sure you gathered, our parents really like Russian names."

He chuckled. "Yeah, I kinda got that. Have they ever been to Russia?"

"Yes. Years ago, my father was in the State Department and did a lot of traveling."

"Interesting. I'd like to hear more about your family," he said.

"Sure. But right now I need to get off the phone. I really need to go to work."

"Okay. Perhaps we can get together later this evening."

"Well, the boys are coming home tonight and I want to spend some time with them. Two days seems like forever."

"Yes, of course," he said quickly. "I understand.

You should be there this evening. I'm sure they missed you."

"Not half as much as I missed them," she said wistfully. "But I had a really good time this weekend. Thank you for everything." Her other line beeped. "My other line—that's probably Mia calling me to tell me the boys are up. I'll talk to you later, okay?" She clicked over to the second line quickly. It wasn't Mia.

"Hi, Mommy," Brice said clearly.

Natalia laughed so hard her cheeks hurt. Hearing her son's voice always sent a thrill of pride and love through her. "Hi, sweetheart. How are you? I miss you," she said. The reply was nonstop chatter. He told her all about his day and that he played with fish and that his uncles took him to play with puppies. The excitement and joy in his voice was contagious. Natalia laughed as he then relayed everything his favorite cartoon character had just done on television. He went on for a few minutes more about making pancakes with Uncle Stephen, then she asked to speak with Jayden. She heard gurgling laughter and then "Dada."

It didn't matter what they said, it only mattered that she heard their voices. After that moment, everything was perfect. As a matter of fact, everything was more than perfect. She relaxed back and had a quick conversation with Mia as she flipped through the day-old mail she'd picked up but never opened Friday evening.

David braced his hands behind his head and felt the warmth of the early-morning sun on his face as he sat out on the balcony. He closed his eyes and thought about his time with Natalia. Spending the night with her was unexpected and amazing. Spending all day Saturday with her in the Bahamas was totally spectacular and Miami was beyond measure. All in all, it was a perfect weekend getaway and sharing it with Natalia made it the best time he'd had in a long time.

He didn't have his guard up with her; he didn't need to. Neither had any illusions as to what they were doing. He knew exactly what she wanted from him and it was nothing he wasn't eagerly willing to give.

Usually he would instinctively be on guard against being used by women with their own agenda—models wanting exposure, actresses seeking a career boost and socialites just wanting to be seen with him on their arm. It was all a game of use-and-be-used.

He'd certainly been with his share of women. They came at him constantly and from every direction. One woman had even broken into his New York apartment and lain naked in his bed, waiting for him. Still another had mailed herself to him in a shipping box and jumped out, wearing only high heels and a grin.

But the thing was, he always saw them for what they were. They wanted what he had and they would do anything to get it. And very often they did. It certainly wasn't all women, but it was enough of them to keep him constantly on alert. That's why he'd come here in the first place. He'd assumed that Natalia was one of those women. He was wrong. He could guard against gold diggers and paternity suits, but how could he protect himself against legitimate fatherhood, even when he hadn't slept with the mother? The legal precedent would be staggering.

Being a movie actor had a way of opening doors—not

to mention other things. But in the few times he'd been with Natalia, no one had touched him as she had. She was passionate, vivacious and spirited. He enjoyed being with her, talking with her and of course making love to her. Being with Natalia showed him just how different a real relationship could be. He liked it.

"There you are," Pamela said as soon as she stepped out onto the balcony. "Good morning. Did you have a good weekend?"

"The best," he said, still smiling.

"Glad to hear it. You look happy."

"I am," he said without opening his eyes. "Deliriously."

"So I guess you already heard the news," Pamela said.

"What news?" he asked, turning to look at her.

"Lenny called. The studio wants to option you for the next two sequels of *Lone Warrior* as soon as possible. You're officially a superhero franchise. Congratulations," she said, smiling.

David sat up instantly. "Seriously?" he said excitedly. She nodded while smiling from ear to ear. "That's fantastic." He sat up, smiled and laughed riotously. "Who would have thought that a postapocalyptic action hero out to save the world would hit such a nerve?"

"Hey, box office receipts don't lie. It's a surprise blockbuster and it's not even summer yet. *Lone Warrior* kicked ass and you know the sequels are gonna be tight. They knew they had to lock you down."

He jumped up, grabbed Pamela and spun her around. She joined in his laughter until her eyes moistened. She thought about her best friend as a tear trembled down her face.

"Brenda would be so…" she began, but didn't finish.

"I know," he said, hugging her close. "I know." They stood a moment thinking about his sister, her best friend. Her death was senseless and the heartbreak of losing her was always just below the surface.

"I have to call Natalia and tell her. She's going to be thrilled."

"Wait. Before you do that, there's more." He stopped and nodded. "Okay, back to business," she said more professionally. "Lenny, by the way, is still on the ceiling. He said that opening at number one in triple-digit receipts last month and staying the number-one movie for three weeks straight really piqued the studio's interest. They didn't want to lose you. Plus, the movie is still pulling in major receipts and it hasn't even gone overseas or onto disk yet. The offer includes executive producer credit and a percentage on the back end. He called you every two hours yesterday. Your cell phone voice mail is loaded."

"I was in Bimini. I'll call him back this afternoon."

"Nope, you gotta make it sooner. They want to see you."

"Who?"

"The studio execs. They want to announce as soon as possible."

"When?"

"Tonight. They're sending the studio jet to meet you right now. Lenny and a couple of execs are on board, finalizing the paperwork. They're picking up a few more cast members in New York and Houston and then they'll do a turnaround back to L.A." She looked at her PDA for confirmation. "They should be here in about five hours."

He nodded. "Anything else?" he asked.

"Yes. We have a situation that needs your attention. Apparently, our tabloid friend, Beck, called the L.A. office for confirmation. Word is that you're donating your 'swimmers' to a clinic for posterity. Apparently, there are women calling clinics all over L.A. asking if it's true. Sounds like he's at least on the right track, but just doesn't know the particulars. My guess is that some big-mouth at the clinic went for the fast cash. So how do you want to handle it?"

"Squash it. I can't have something like that coming out now. Technically, the story is incorrect. Just tell them that I am not now and have no intention in the future of donating sperm to any bank."

She nodded and began typing in a text message. "Got it. I'll use that exact quote."

"Is that it?" he asked.

"Yep, for now. You need to get packed."

"Do me a favor. Get me a few books on parenting." Pam looked at him questioningly and then smiled and shook her head. "No editorializing. Just do it," he said, not wanting to hear her commentary.

"Sure. Any particular ones?"

"Anything's fine. No, wait. Find me something on toddlers and preschoolers—from a father's perspective, if possible."

"Sure," she nodded. "Anything else?"

"Yeah, send a couple of bouquets of flowers to the

spa downstairs—attention Natalia and Nikita Coles. No note. That's it. Get Lenny on the phone before you go," he requested. Pam nodded, picked up his cell and dialed. A few seconds later, David was speaking with his very excited agent.

Chapter 11

Natalia pulled up in front of her sister's home and got out of the car. As soon as she climbed the steps, the screen door opened. Nikita stood in the doorway with a cup in her hands. "Okay, lady, you'd better have a good reason for getting me up this early on my day off. Our spa appointment isn't for another few hours."

"I do. Trust me," Natalia said.

"Come on in," Nikita said as her sister approached.

"Good morning," Natalia said, reaching the last step. Nikita handed the cup to her as she walked inside. Natalia headed straight to the kitchen. Nikita followed.

"Umm, what smells so good?" Natalia asked.

As usual, Nikita was baking, and whatever she had in the oven smelled heavenly. Natalia stood at the counter as Nikita walked over to the sink and washed her hands. She grabbed some paper towels, then picked up a colander of freshly washed berries and brought it to where Natalia sat.

"I'm trying out a few new recipes for the bakery. I've got some turkey potpies in the oven."

"Umm, they smell incredible. My mouth is watering."

"Good, that's exactly the effect I was hoping for."

"And what is this going to be?" Natalia asked of the bowl on the counter filled with cubed white cake topped with what looked like a crème brûlée mixture.

"A very berry sweet-bread pudding, if all goes well," she said as she opened the oven and pulled out a tray of small pastry-covered goodies. The aroma wafting from the open oven made Natalia's mouth water all over again. Nikita grabbed oven mitts, placed each small dish on an oven grate, then turned to Natalia. "All right now. What's going on with you?"

"I got this in the mail."

Nikita looked at the already opened letter, then up at her sister. "What is it?"

"I messed up," Natalia said, then simply handed her sister an envelope.

Nikita pulled the letter out and quickly read through it. A smile lit up her face and brightened as she continued reading. "Are you kidding? You did it. You're a finalist for the grant," she squealed, hurrying around the counter to hug her. "Congratulations! I'm so proud of you. This is fantastic news. What are you talking about—you messed up? This is fantastic."

"Not quite. I went out to dinner with David Friday night," she confessed.

"To celebrate the news?"

"No, I didn't open the letter until this morning."

"So what? You went out—like on a date?" Nikita asked.

Natalia half nodded. "More like a just-hanging-out thing."

"Get out, for real?" Nikita said even more gleefully than before. Natalia shrugged. "Well, what's wrong with that? You're both single, mature adults. How was it, how was he?"

"Niki," Natalia began. "There's more."

"More? Oh, my goodness. Tatiana is going to faint when she hears this. Okay, details—I want details," Nikita demanded.

Natalia paused and looked away. "One thing led to another, then we…"

"Whoa, whoa! What do you mean, one thing lead to another?"

"You know exactly what I mean," she said, looking at her sister knowingly. Nikita's jaw dropped open. "It was impulsive and mind-blowing and totally out-of-this-world amazing. But now in the light of day I'm thinking, how is he ever going to take me or the center seriously now? I don't know what I was thinking." She shook her head miserably. "I take that back. I wasn't thinking at all."

"You mean like with the photograph."

"What photograph?" Natalia asked.

"This photograph," Nikita said, handing her a printed paper.

"What's this?"

"It's a photo of movie star David Montgomery strolling down the pristine streets of Bimini Saturday afternoon with an unidentified woman. Tell me—does the woman in the picture look familiar to you or is it just me?" Nikita asked. Natalia instantly grabbed the paper and looked at it. Her jaw dropped.

"So I gather from your stunned expression and the way your cheeks just flushed that it was you."

"Yes, it's me."

"No kidding," she said rhetorically as she buttered and sugared two small dessert ramekins.

"I can't believe this. Where'd you get this?"

"Tatiana sent it to me."

"Tatiana is in London. How did she get it?"

"A photographer friend of hers sent it to her joking that if he hadn't just seen her earlier that night he would have added her name to the photo for publication."

"Wait. They can't publish this," Natalia exclaimed.

"Honey, it's David Montgomery with a new woman on his arm. Of course they can. They already have."

"No, wait. They need my approval and I won't give it."

"Wake up, Natalia. David Montgomery is in the public domain and that means anyone associated with him is also fair game. Believe me, the paparazzi for some of these magazines don't wait around to get signed releases. They print first and ask questions later. As you can see, they don't have your name yet, but when they do…"

"Yeah, I know. I'm screwed. I need to talk to David." She stepped down from the stool and grabbed her purse.

"No, no, no. First you need to tell me what's going on." She sat back down and looked at Nikita, not knowing where to begin. "To tell you the truth, that's a good question. I don't exactly know. We kissed Friday and everything changed after that. We had dinner on his boat, then it was off to Bimini and Miami, then..." She paused and shook her head. "I didn't plan it. It just happened—and happened and happened a few more times."

Nikita smiled and chuckled. "Well, needless to say I'm thrilled for you. There's nothing like an intense physical attraction to release pent-up sexual energy. And sweetie, you so needed to release all that sexual energy. So, in my opinion, it's about time you had a little fun in your life."

"Fun," she said, shaking her head fretfully. "I have no idea what I'm doing. I mean this was just one Friday night dinner and it turned into Saturday afternoon in Bimini and Saturday night in Miami. And now this." She motioned to the photo. Natalia shook her head again miserably.

"Nat, the man's a major movie star. He's got a blockbuster movie out in theaters right now. Of course the media's interested in him. And, in case you hadn't noticed, he's rich, famous and gorgeous. That means a lot of other people are interested in him, too."

"I must be out of my mind to be getting myself involved with him. But the thing is—I really like him. He's kind and generous and funny and he makes he feel like I really matter. I know I'm just a fling to him and I shouldn't get emotionally involved, but he's so easy to fall for. He's the wrong man at the wrong time."

"What are you talking about? This is the best thing to happen to you in a long time. Sweetie, only a sister would tell you this, but your dating drought has gone critical. Did it ever occur to you that he's the right man at the right time?"

"None of this matters anymore anyway," Natalia said, shaking her head. "After last weekend I can't even think about accepting the grant money. It would be wrong."

"Wrong? Come on, Nat. You did the right thing to apply for the grant. You worked for weeks to get the application just right and complete the process. You said yourself that his foundation was a perfect fit and he must think so, too, or else he wouldn't be here, right?"

Natalia sighed. "I wasn't thinking."

"You're right—you were feeling. Nat, you're always thinking for others. When people get in trouble, you're the first person everyone calls. You're the family shrink. I say it's about time you have a little fun."

"You don't understand. I can't accept this money now."

"Why not?"

"It would make me just like Clay Sullivan."

"How? Sullivan is a sleazeball who wanted you to sleep with him to get his foundation grant. You refused. Did David put that kind of stipulation on his grant, too?"

"No."

"Then I don't see the problem."

"What Clay did was disgusting and if I take this, I'll be just as corrupt as he is. If people found out what I did, the center will have zero credibility. It's like I slept with him for a reason and you know what that makes me."

To Nikita's blank stare, Natalia continued. "I slept with David, then this letter comes. Don't you see?"

"If you're referring to what I think you're referring to, I think you're way off base. One thing has nothing to do with the other. Tell me, did you sleep with him to win the grant?"

"Niki, I slept with the man and then I got a finalist letter for over a half-million-dollar grant. Don't you think that smacks of deceit, fraud, ethical misrepresentation, maybe even conspiracy?"

"No, not at all. If you win the grant, I say accept it graciously. You need the money, the kids need the money. Take it."

"I can't. It wouldn't feel right. I'll find the money some other way."

"So what about your relationship with David?" she asked.

Natalia shrugged. "I can't have photos of myself flashed around like this. I have children to protect. It's over."

"With him that's probably easier said than done."

"No. I can handle this. I'll simply end it before it gets too complicated." She stood to leave.

"My opinion? It's already complicated," Nikita said.

Natalia looked back at her sister, knowing that she wasn't far from the truth. "Can we rain-check the spa today?" Natalia asked. Nikita nodded. Natalia turned and left. She knew what she had to do. She got into the car and headed into town.

David stood waiting. As soon as the elevator doors opened, he smiled happily. The sight of her was exactly what he needed. Plus, he couldn't wait to tell her about the new movie deal. "This is a lovely surprise. Come on in." He escorted her to his suite, then followed her inside. As soon as he closed the door, he grabbed her back into his arms and held her close. "Umm, you smell good." He kissed her quickly then released her.

"Thanks," she said, hoping not to waver in her resolve to end their relationship.

"I'm glad you stopped by. I missed you." He leaned in to kiss her again. She turned slightly and he kissed her cheek. "Are you okay? Are the boys okay? You missed your spa appointment."

"How did you know about that?" Natalia asked.

"I sent flowers, but was told that you had canceled."

"I'm fine. We're all fine," she said, moving away from him.

"Good. Have a seat. Can I get you something to drink?"

"No, thanks. I'm good. I can't stay. I just wanted to ask you about…" She paused, seeing the suitcase sitting beside the sofa for the first time. Her stomach jumped. "You're leaving," she concluded.

He smiled. "I need to take care of some business for a few days. I should be back before the end of the week."

She nodded. "Have a good trip."

"Thanks. Wish you were coming with me," he suggested openly with the smile that made him famous.

"Umm, this came this morning." She pulled an envelope from her purse and handed it to him.

"A letter?" he asked without taking it.

"A registered letter from the Montgomery Foundation. My application was approved. I'm one of the finalists for the grant."

He smiled happily. "Congratulations! That's great. We need to celebrate," he said, walking over to the desk and picking up the phone.

"No, wait," she said, stopping him by placing her hand on the phone and easing it back down into the cradle.

He looked at her, questioning. "What's wrong?"

"You did this, didn't you?"

"Yes."

"Why?"

"Because you need the grant money," he said simply.

"No, you can't just arbitrarily make a phone call and make money available like that."

He smiled. "Actually, I can. You need it, and I facilitated it."

"It's wrong."

He looked at her, confused. "What are you talking about? The grant's not enough? You need more money?"

"No, no. The grant's amazing. It couldn't be more perfect. It's just that I let this get personal and that was a mistake."

"A mistake how, Natalia?" he asked, fearing that he'd been played.

"This, the grant, the money, I can't take it."

"You're turning it down?" he asked. She nodded. "Why?"

"Because it looks like quid pro quo," she said. "I

allowed this to be personal and that was wrong. I jeopardized the center." She offered him the envelope back. He looked at it, but didn't take it. She placed it on the desk and turned to leave.

"Natalia, wait. You can't be serious."

"I'm very serious," she said firmly.

"So that's it?" he asked.

"I'm sorry. You have no idea how sorry I am, but I can't accept the grant. I crossed the line and it will look bad for both of us if this goes public. Both the foundation's credibility and mine would be called into question. I can't do that, no matter how much we need the money."

"So because we slept together you're giving this back?" he asked. She nodded. "Why? Are you feeling guilty about something?" She smiled and nodded. His heart nearly stilled. "Is that what it was from the beginning, Natalia—coercion and seduction for money? You had to know I was going to intercede with the foundation on your behalf."

She glared at him hard. "No, I didn't know, and don't confuse me with the others. I'm not one of them. Friday and Saturday had nothing to do with who or what you are. It had to do with a man and a woman being together. But with this letter, business got personal and it shouldn't have. It looks wrong and you know it, too."

"So you're saying that the man and the woman part had nothing to do with the grant," he asked, glancing down at the envelope on the desk.

"You know it didn't."

"No, I don't," he said plainly.

They stared at each other a moment longer, then

she turned and walked to the front door. She opened it and paused when he called out her name. "So none of this—what happened between us meant anything to you?" he asked. She didn't say anything. He knew that instant that she was holding back her feelings. "It did, didn't it? But still you're willing to push me away, for appearances' sake?"

"Have a good trip," she said, then closed the door behind her.

David stood wondering what had just happened.

Chapter 12

Days later, Natalia walked down the hall of the teen center, then peeked into the nursery room. Several children sat with coloring sheets and large bulky crayons, including her son, Brice. His head was down and he was intently focused on whatever he was coloring. Natalia smiled. He was such an inquisitive child. He loved drawing, painting, coloring and playing make-believe. His imagination was limitless. He also loved being the center of attention.

She saw Jayden asleep in one of the cribs, then stepped away from the side window and continued walking toward the storage closet. Her phone rang just as she got to the door. She stopped, looked at the caller ID and then answered. It was Nikita. "Hey."

"He's on his way back to town," she said simply.

Natalia knew exactly who her sister was talking about, but still her heart jumped. "I heard. I can handle it."

"Are you sure?"

"Truthfully, no."

"At least you're not kidding yourself. Have you heard anything from him lately?"

"He called dozens of times, but I didn't take the calls. We said everything we needed to say to each other the last time."

"I'm sorry."

"Niki, it's okay. It's for the best, really. I'm fine. Let's face it—he's who he is and I'm me. It was one weekend, a nice fantasy. That's all."

"No, it wasn't."

"Would you please allow me to rationalize?" Natalia scolded.

"Feel like company tonight?"

"No, thanks. I'm taking the boys on a picnic and to the playground. Hopefully, with all the fun, they'll be exhausted by the time we get home so I can catch up on my paperwork."

"Sounds good. If you need me, call."

"I will. Talk to you later."

Natalia closed her cell, then unlocked and opened the storage closet door. The fluorescent lights flickered as soon as she turned them on. The closet was small, dark and nearly empty. She stepped inside and leaned back against the door frame. Her heart thundered and her stomach twirled. David was coming back to town. He'd said a few days, but he'd been gone over a week. He had called and left messages a few times, but she refused to reply. She sighed heavily, having decided that thinking about him was a waste of time and effort. She looked up at the empty shelves, grabbed two packs of white copy paper, closed the door and headed back to the computer room. Her cell rang again. It was Mia at the front desk. "Hey."

"Nat, you're wanted up front."

"Okay, I'll be there in a minute," Natalia said, presuming it was the same problem they generally had. People would walk in off the street thinking that the facility was a soup kitchen. She usually gave them a few coupons or a few dollars for a meal.

"Ms. Coles, Ms. Coles."

Natalia turned and saw two of her teenagers running to catch up with her. "Denise, Shanna, slow down, slow down. What's wrong?"

"Um, oh, my God, Ms. Coles," Denise said, barely catching her breath. "You are never gonna guess who's waiting out in the reception area for you."

"He is so sexy gorgeous. I swear I wanted to jump him right there. You feelin' me?" Shanna said, holding her hand up for her friend to agree with her.

"I know that's right," Denise said, slapping Shanna's hand. "Yeah, a'ight, now that's what I'm talkin' 'bout, and he's got deep pockets and everything about him was sexy."

"Ladies," Natalia said, looking at the teens sternly.

"A'ight, we know, we know. First rule: be respectful of self and others."

"Exactly. Do you want to try that again?" Natalia asked.

"A'ight. Mrs. Morales asked us to find you and tell you that David Montgomery's waiting in the office."

Shanna nodded eagerly. "He asked for you personally.

I didn't know you had it like that, knowing movie stars and all. What's up?"

"Oh, my God, I just saw his movie last week. It is so good."

"I saw it three times already. I didn't know you knew movie stars. Pharrell is in it, and he's too gorgeous."

"Do you think you can ask him if he can get Pharrell to come and perform here at the center? We can blow it up in here and get all kinds of cash coming in."

"Thank you, ladies. Do me a favor and take this paper to the computer lab," Natalia said, turning to head back to the front of the building. Several kids were also headed in that direction.

As soon as she got to the open doorway of the reception area, she saw a crowd of teens and kids all laughing and talking, surrounding David on all sides. The girls were right—he was sexy gorgeous. He wore a simple white shirt with straight-leg jeans, and everything about him was sexy. The kids took pictures with cell phones and got his autograph, all while calling out questions and comments. David was answering, apparently loving every minute of it. Mia walked up beside Natalia, smiling. "Looks like they're having a great time," Mia said, watching the impromptu interview session.

"Yeah, looks like," Natalia said, obviously troubled.

"I gather his arrival here today is a surprise to you."

"Absolutely. A complete surprise," Natalia said.

David glanced over and saw Natalia standing by the door. He smiled, then nodded once. Natalia nodded back. Mia, watching their interaction, began clapping her hands to get everyone's attention. "All right, guys. Let's wrap it up and get back to what we were doing. We'll let Mr. Montgomery and Ms. Coles have a minute." There was a collective groan of disapproval. "I'm sure that's not how we want Mr. Montgomery to think we behave here, is it?"

The kids slowly began leaving the room, ushered by Mia with an ever-watchful eye on Natalia as she moved to the inner office. When the last student left, Mia showed David into the office area then stood smiling at the two of them until the awkwardness of the moment hit her.

"Okay, insert definite uncomfortable moment here. I'll check on the computer-room drama for you," Mia said before winking and closing the door behind her.

"Hi," Natalia said as her stomach quivered again.

David's sexy half smile creased the one dimple in his chiseled jaw. "Hi, yourself," he said in his most decidedly masculine voice. He exhaled slowly as he looked down the length of her luscious body. He removed his dark sunglasses and licked his lips seductively. He took in her navy blue flared skirt, navy blue zippered sleeveless sweater and navy heels, accented with pearls.

Natalia felt his eyes on her. Her stomach lurched and her skin goose-pimpled instantly. "Welcome back," she said as calmly as she could, hoping to gain some control over her wayward nerves.

"Thanks. Wow, you look good enough to eat." His smile changed to a more devilish, purposeful grin. The very real thought of walking over and making love to her right there in her office made his body react. "I've been thinking about you, about us."

"Oh, I forgot. Congratulations on your success. I saw that you've signed to do a couple of sequels. That's great."

"Thanks. I also got another role," he said.

"Really, that's wonderful. What's the role?"

"I play a man who falls for a woman and can't get her out of his mind. The thing is, he has no idea why she won't answer or return his phone calls. She completely shuts him off. He's been waiting for a long time to find someone like her and right now he can't stop thinking about her or their time together."

She sighed. "David, there's nothing to think about. We had a great weekend, that's all."

"Is that all you want it to be?"

"That's what it has to be."

He moved closer and took her hand, pulling her into his arms. "That's not all it was."

She looked up into his eyes and nodded. "That's all it can be."

"Then why can't I stop thinking about you?" he asked softly. She looked away. "I'd be doing an interview and suddenly I'm wondering what you ate for dinner or if your son bumped his head again, or why can't I have you in my life."

She looked back at him and smiled slowly. "It's for the best."

He nodded. "Mia, your associate, is she the same Mia who babysat a few weeks ago?" he asked. Natalia nodded, thankful that he changed the subject. "She's nice. I like her. She told me that you were cousins."

"Mia married my cousin, Esteban, last year. She was actually a college professor in Atlanta, but now she works here at the center. After she moved here, she decided that she didn't want to go back to teaching college, so I asked her to help out. She agreed. The kids love her. She's completely dedicated and the only full-time volunteer worker. I don't know what we'd do without her."

"Before you came out, Mia updated me about the center. It looked great on paper, but actually being here—seeing and talking with the kids—I have to say I'm more impressed than ever. You've done an incredible job here. Natalia, you deserve that grant."

"I'm currently making other arrangements."

"Which are?"

"The center is going in a more public-donation direction. My family and I will be donating the bulk of the money needed to sustain operations."

"Is that what you want to do?" he asked.

"To take money from my family?" she asked. He nodded. "No, but it will keep the center doors open at least until the end of the year, and that's the important thing," she said.

"After that, what happens next year?"

"I'll figure something out."

He nodded his admiration and pride, then smiled at her. "You look great," David said, moving close.

Natalia swallowed hard then walked over to one of the desks. Her stomach did a somersault as her heart slammed against her chest repeatedly. He had her nerves jumping and her senses on overdrive. She watched as he walked over to the other desk and picked up the frame.

It was an LCD and the picture continuously changed. "These are photographs of your sons?"

"Yes, that's them."

"They're older here than on your cell phone."

She nodded. "They grow up fast," she said, peering over his shoulder at the photograph. "These are the most recent, so they're about that size. They're in the ninetieth percentile for their age and weight."

"What are they doing at this age?" David asked, remembering some of the things he'd read in the parenting books.

"Jayden is ten months old. He's cruising and getting into everything. He does peek-a-boo and patty-cake and he's usually very happy. Just seeing him makes you want to smile. He doesn't talk exactly, just two-syllable babbling like *mama*. He's learning some independence and he's feeding himself. His dexterity is improving hourly. Plus," she added with a broad smile, "he's stubborn—very stubborn."

"What about Brice?"

"Now, he's the character. He's such a little ham. But I know you didn't come here to ask me about my sons. So what are you doing here?"

"I came for a tour of the facility."

"David, I don't have time to play games."

"I'm not playing games. Your center's brochure said that tours are available on a walk-in basis."

"That's for those interested in our program and our services and the last I heard you don't have any children."

"Not everything is as it seems," he said cryptically.

She looked at him. "What do you mean?"

"The tour is also for interested professionals, correct?" She nodded. "Well, I'm an interested professional. Show me the center. I want to see all this through your eyes."

Her shoulders slumped as she relented. She had no choice but to give him a tour.

"Our mission here is to give area kids a safe place to go and have fun while also learning. We try to make this a loving, caring environment. Our volunteers are teachers, church members, public officials and business professionals. Each volunteer undergoes a stringent background check, which is updated yearly. We want our children to be safe here. This facility is basically an alternative to the streets. We ask each parent or guardian to volunteer a few hours once a week."

"Sounds good," he said. "Shall we begin our tour?"

He stepped aside and Natalia led the way back through the reception area then down the hall to the main center. There were students in the hall and some in classrooms. "This is it. Most of the participants are in classes right now." She described the different programs and courses. They stopped periodically so that Natalia could introduce David to volunteer staff members, but mostly she kept the tour moving quickly.

"Right now we're open only three days a week— Thursday, Friday and Saturday. We have a staff of six volunteers and my family helps out a lot. We go on field trips and take the older kids to ball games and on college tours and things like that. I primarily deal with the younger kids."

"How do they get here—walk or catch a bus?" he asked.

"The school bus drops them off when school's in session. In the summer the parents drop them off in the morning and pick them up by seven in the evening."

"Impressive. Is there payment involved?"

"We're nonprofit, so we don't actually get paid. We depend on foundation grants and only charge on a sliding scale. The city and state have been very generous in the past." She decided to omit the part that their assistance would no longer be forthcoming.

"We have a lounge area, which is mostly for our preteens and teens," she continued. "There are video games, television, music and other entertainment activities. We also have teen tutoring, mentoring and college-prep programs in the computer lab. The only requirement is for them to maintain a good academic standing in school."

"And the younger children?" he asked.

"They're down the hall here—middle school on one side and elementary school on the other. Fun learning is our top priority. My aunt was a schoolteacher and she set up the incredible programs we now follow."

"Is she here at the center? I'd like to meet her."

"No, she owns and operates day-care centers in Marathon, Florida."

"This place is really amazing. Two stories, it's a lot larger than I expected. I can see why you love it. I can also see you all over here. It's warm and inviting. How do you do all this plus work as a social worker for the city and raise two boys?"

"I manage," she said.

"You were wrong. You are most definitely Wonder Woman," he said softly.

"We had planned on starting a parenting skills program this summer. It's something we've been trying to launch for some time now. We'll be implementing that next year."

"What's stopping you from starting it this summer?"

"Our finances are…"

"Take the grant, Natalia," David insisted.

She turned to him. "You know I can't do that."

"Because we slept together or because you're sabotaging your success here?" She looked up at him, then looked away. He'd obviously gotten her attention. "It looks to me like the center could use the money. What do you have—some kind of code-of-conduct rule around here?" he asked.

She turned to him. "Yes, there is a code of conduct and that means that I can't sleep with a man who then gives me money."

"Somehow I don't think this code applies to two single, mature adults."

"It's a code of conduct I have for myself."

"Is this about you and Clay Sullivan?" he asked. She looked at him, surprised. "Yeah, I know about that. As I said before, my assistant is very good at what she does. This isn't the same thing. Neither one of us intended this to happen. There were no plans or preconceived notions. Natalia, I'm not him. I would never hurt you like that."

She looked at him, but didn't say anything. He quietly

pulled her over to the side. "Why are you punishing the center because you have needs?"

She moved away and continued walking down the hall. "We'll be implementing the parenting skills program in the fall," she said, continuing with the tour—all business.

"Will you be teaching the parenting skills program?"

"No," she said. Then she led him into the tiny-tots room. A small boy ran up to her as soon as she entered. He had a crayon-covered drawing and was excitedly telling her about what he had done. Then he looked up, seeing David smiling down at him. Natalia looked at David.

"Hi," Brice said. "Wanna see my picture, too?"

"Yes, I'd love to see it." David knelt down to be on Brice's eye level, just as the parenting books suggested. "Did you color all this?" he asked.

Brice nodded exuberantly. "And I did all this, too. I like to draw. This is a tree like me."

"David, this is my son Brice. Brice, this is a friend, Mr. Montgomery."

"We're going to the playground. Wanna come?"

"No," Natalia spoke up quickly. "Sweetie, Mr. Montgomery is a very busy man. I'm sure he doesn't have time to hang out at the park with us."

"Why not?" Brice asked him.

David smiled. "You know what, Brice? I'd love to hang out at the park with you," he said, smiling at his son. "Do you think Jayden will want to come, too?"

He nodded his head vigorously. "Uh-huh. He likes the slide when Mommy goes down with him. I can go down the slide by myself. He's over there in the little baby crib."

David turned around, seeing a little face peeking above a mesh screen playpen. He was laughing and jumping up and down. He tossed a plastic ball then squealed with delight, repeating the action next with a plastic square. Natalia walked over to pick up the toys and his eyes lit up as he looked up at her. His smile brightened even more. David's heart melted, realizing for the first time that there was no way he could walk away from his sons, his family. It didn't matter how they were conceived; they were his and that was all that mattered now.

Natalia picked Jayden up and stood him on the floor in front of her. He held on to her legs a second then let go. He wobbled at first and then he got his balance and went toddling over to Brice. He got halfway there then plopped down on his butt and crawled the rest of the way. "He's a baby," Brice whispered loudly close to David's ear. "He falls a lot. It's okay. He doesn't get hurt a lot." When Jayden got to him, Brice gave Jayden his crayon. Natalia walked over quickly to take it away, but David eased it away from him first. They looked at each other. She nodded appreciatively, and he smiled.

"Do you like my mommy?" Brice asked.

David smiled and nodded while looking up at Natalia. "Yes, Brice, I like your mommy a whole lot. I love your mommy."

Natalia looked at him without responding.

"Cross your heart?" Brice asked, crossing his chest with his little fingers.

"Yes."

"No, that's not the way you gotta supposed to do it. Mommy says that if you really, really mean it you have to do this, too." He took David's hand and crossed his finger over his heart.

David smiled and nodded. "You know what? Your mommy is a very smart lady and she's absolutely right. Yes, I love your mommy. Cross my heart," he said, repeating the action of crossing his heart while looking up at her.

Then David felt the tug of Jayden pulling up on him as Brice grabbed hold of him, too. He stood with both boys in his arms. His heart nearly burst with joy. He looked at Natalia and smiled. "Ready to go to the playground?" he said excitedly, anxious to spend the evening with his family.

Natalia nodded. How could she not?

Chapter 13

As soon as they stepped outside, there was an ominous roll of thunder in the distance. David looked at Natalia, questioning their next move. She shook her head and shrugged. It was obvious that the evening's activities would have to be postponed.

"It looks like we're going have to take a rain check on the picnic and playground idea this evening," she said. He nodded slowly. Clearly, this was the last thing he wanted to hear. By the time she strapped the boys into their car seats, it had begun to drizzle. The picnic and playground idea was officially abandoned.

"It's raining," she said needlessly.

"Yes, it is."

She looked back to the two-story building then up at the gray sky. "I guess we'd better say goodbye. Thanks for helping me load the car."

"You're welcome."

"Well, we'd better get home. The boys are probably hungry."

He nodded. "Probably."

"Okay." She shrugged. "I'll see you later." She turned toward the driver's door. David stopped her and spun her around. Before she could think or speak, he kissed her. She held tight as her mind spun in a million different directions. When the kiss ended she leaned back against the wet car as he opened the driver's door for her. She got in and drove home just as the rain began to come down. Jayden fell asleep and Brice had on his toddler headphones, listening to his music.

"See you soon," David said watching the car exit the small parking lot.

Natalia pulled into her garage just as lightning streaked across the sky. The sound of thunder roared closer as the rain started pouring down heavier. The boys were anxious, so she held them tight reassuring them as they hurried inside. With less drama than expected, she got them settled in the house and was just about to start dinner when her doorbell rang. She hurried, knowing that whoever was there was outside getting soaked. She opened the door to see David soaking wet. "David, what are you doing here?" she asked.

He held up a picnic basket. "I thought we could have our picnic inside," he sputtered.

She chuckled and hurried him into the house. He dripped everywhere.

"I can't believe you came back out in this weather. That's insane. We usually have flash floods when it storms like this."

"Yeah, I know. I just drove through one. The water was nearly halfway up the side of my car door."

"You're wet. Did you just take a bath outside? What's that?" Brice asked, seeing David standing in the foyer, soaking wet.

"This is a picnic basket," he said.

"We can't have a picnic, 'cause it's raining out. Mommy says no picnic in the rain."

"Mommy's right. But I had a better idea, if Mommy says it's okay." Both Brice and David turned to her.

"Brice," Natalia began, "Mr. Montgomery thought that it would be nice to have our picnic inside. What do you think?" Brice nodded and squealed excitedly, then immediately ran to tell Jayden that the picnic was still on.

"This is very sweet of you."

"I'm going out of town again tomorrow. I couldn't let my boys down."

"Come on, I'll get you some of my brother's dry clothes. He left them here the last time he helped with the yard. Then we can set up the picnic in the den." David followed her upstairs to her bedroom. There was a large canopy bed pushed against the far wall.

David watched her leave then walked over to the bedroom's fireplace. There were beautiful black-and-white photos of Brice and Jayden playing together and also a baby picture of each at birth. He picked up the photos and smiled, touching the glass gently.

She handed him a neat pile of clothes and towels. "Okay, you're all set. Just come downstairs when you're done."

"Where's the den?"

She smiled and chuckled. "Just follow the noise."

In the den, she gathered picnic essentials and piled them together to create the perfect atmosphere. When David walked in, he found a huge blanket spread out in the center of the floor and a colorful tent placed in the corner with two large ficus and hibiscus trees placed just behind it. There was a scattering of stuffed animals, and wild animal sounds filled the room.

Natalia was sitting on the blanket with Jayden crawling and toddling into her arms. David paused in the doorway and smiled, overjoyed by the welcoming family scene. This was what his life was supposed to be like. This was his family. He gazed at Natalia, playing with his younger son. He'd known her for only a few weeks, but they were worth a lifetime as far as he was concerned. When he looked at her, he saw what he was missing, what he wanted, his future. She was the woman he'd been searching for all his life. But he knew that telling her why he'd originally come to Key West would break her heart.

Natalia looked up when he appeared in the doorway. He looked like he belonged there. She realized right then that she was lost. She'd fallen in love. "Hi, we decided to go with a safari theme."

"It looks fantastic," David said, smiling and chuckling. "Perfect."

Brice poked his head out through the flap of the tent and called David to come inside. He did. It thundered, stormed and rained outside, but the safari picnic inside was the best ever. The next two hours were spent eating, playing games, telling stories and loving every minute. David was in the middle of a story when Brice fell asleep on his lap. "I think he's had just about enough fun for one day," David said.

"Here, I'll put him to bed," she said, grabbing a warmed bottle of milk for Jayden, who was cranky and fighting to stay awake.

"May I help?" he asked, holding Brice close and gently patting his back to soothe him.

"Sure," Natalia answered gratefully.

Together they put Brice into his toddler bed, then David went back to the den to start cleaning up. He folded the tent and blanket and placed the stuffed animals on the sofa. He rinsed, then placed the dirty dishes in the dishwasher and put the rest of the food in the refrigerator. He turned the animal music off then went up to the boys' room again. He stood in the doorway and watched as Natalia, having rocked Jayden to sleep, placed him into his crib and tucked Brice in again.

He couldn't resist smiling at the perfect scene. Natalia kissed their foreheads and said good night silently. She turned, seeing David smiling at her from across the room. Motioning for his silence, they went back downstairs into the den. She began picking up toys and blocks and books. David started chuckling to himself when he picked up a book. He'd read Brice the book seven times. "Brice really loves this book. Looks like you're gonna need a new one pretty soon."

Natalia looked up with an armful of stuffed animals. "It's his favorite book *this* month. The thing is, he'll have a new favorite in a few weeks. Last month he couldn't live without *Goodnight Moon*. The month before that it was *The Little Engine That Could* and *Star Light*."

When all the toys had been put away in the toy box in the den's window seat, David and Natalia went back into the living room. "Natalia, the boys—they're absolutely perfect."

She smiled. "Not quite, but they're really good boys." She walked over to the mantel above the fireplace and picked a double picture frame with both boys' baby photos. She handed it to David.

"I don't know what to say. You're an incredible mother. You're caring and kind—everything a mother should be. Seeing you with them and seeing the love and trust in their eyes is inspiring," he said, holding the frame as if it were a precious treasure.

"Thank you. Some days are harder than others, but being their mother for me is the single most incredible job in the world."

"You do it well, and I'm totally amazed by your dedication and compassion." He reluctantly handed the frame back to her. She put it back on the mantel.

"You were pretty good yourself tonight. Jayden is a very picky eater and he actually ate all his food for you. You fed him sweet potatoes and peas—he hates peas. But he ate them for you. That's amazing. You're going to be a great dad someday."

"I never thought I'd ever have children. I never even considered it until recently."

"Wait, you want kids? I thought I remembered reading an interview with you saying that you're not the fatherly type."

"I guess I was wrong. I never knew my father, and my mother, well, let's just say I have trust issues when it comes to mothers because of her." He smiled at her. "You changed all that."

"We don't have to be the type of parents our parents were." She walked over to the sofa and sat. He sat beside her. "I have a friend whose mother beat her and her sisters repeatedly when they were growing up. She grew up fearful and terrified of a lot of things. My friend now refuses to a lay a hand on her own children. As a result, her children are well-adjusted and happy. Ultimately, we make our own choices and follow what we think is right. My mom and dad were great parents, but I'm raising my boys my way."

"You're doing a wonderful job," he assured her. "Except whose idea was it to get him a rolling popping toy? It's so loud."

She laughed. "That would be my brother Mikhail. He gave it to Brice a few years ago. Now Jayden plays with it nonstop. He loves the loud noise it makes."

He laughed at the memory of Jayden and the toy.

"Don't let them fool you, David. They're not always so nice and polite; they're boys and brothers. Brice sometimes realizes that Jayden is a baby and treats him accordingly; other times he wants Jayden to play with him as if they're the same age. That's why he attends nursery school. There he plays and interacts with kids his own age. He enjoys that. It makes him feel like a big guy." She smiled. "That is, when he's not causing a riot."

"A riot? What do you mean?" he asked. She told him a story about one of Brice's more exuberant moments. They laughed, enjoying the energy and spirit of his actions. "He's a great kid. They both are. What do you do when you can't be here? Do you have a nanny?"

"No."

"Do you need one?"

"No, not exactly my style," she said.

"Do you need anything, I mean for the boys? I can take care of private school, clothes, lessons, college. I can even…"

"Stop—enough! What is this really?" she asked.

"What is what? What do you mean?"

"I mean since day one, you've had some kind of agenda when it comes to me. You walked into my office for a reason. Since you and I don't have a past in common, I can only assume there's something in the present that concerns me. I've tried to let it go, for purely selfish reasons, but I need to know before this gets any more complicated. There's something else going on here, isn't there?" she asked. He didn't respond. "What is it?"

"What do you mean?" he asked innocently, his expression pinched and curious.

"Wow, now that had to be the absolute worst line you've ever delivered," she said, then stood up and headed for the kitchen.

He grabbed her arm to stop her. "Natalia, wait," he said. She turned back to him. He looked into her eyes and knew that there was no way he could tell her what he knew he had to. His heart wouldn't let him. He loved her and nothing else mattered to him anymore. But he knew that she would feel differently. It would surely matter to her.

"You're right. There is something else. But you're not ready to hear it."

"And you think that you can make that call for me? If it concerns me—and it obviously does—then you need to tell me."

He walked away and stood at the bay window. The curtains were open and he looked up at the ominous sky. Heavy, overgrown trees obscured his view, but he knew dark clouds and heavy rain lay beyond the obstructions. Thunder continued to rumble in the distance as he thought and considered his words carefully. "Ever since I was thirteen, I've been on my own. I learned the streets young and was smart enough to stay ahead of the drugs, gangs and other drama. I learned to depend on myself and trust no one. In Compton, I had little choice. Not a lot has changed since then. I was still that thirteen-year-old, mistrusting boy when I arrived here a few weeks ago."

"And now you're not?" she asked.

"Brenda, my sister, was the trusting one. She believed in people—their basic goodness. Even when she saw such ugliness around us, she believed. I always thought that that made her weak, but I see now that she was the strong one—not me. She always told me that people weren't as bad if you give them a chance. I never did. When she died, she took that trust and belief with her. Once I became famous, I saw that I was right. Everybody wants something from me—the fans, the media and the studio—everybody. Except you." He turned and looked at her as if seeing her for the first time.

Natalia allowed him to talk freely. She knew that he

needed to rationalize his feelings and understand that not everyone stood against him.

"Trust," he began again as he turned away. "I could never understand that until I came here. I lived my life through my career, the characters I play. I never expected to have a family or children. That way I never needed or allowed myself to trust anyone." He turned back to her. "Then you came along. You want to know what all this is about. It's about me finding my life, my real life, here, in this place. I don't want to lose what I found here." He studied her reaction as she moved closer.

She stood in front of him. "You won't lose it. You're not alone anymore, David," she said. "I'm here whenever you need me."

David wrapped his arm around her waist, holding her close, then reaching up to stroke the side of her face lovingly. "Natalia, you've turned my world upside down. I'm always gonna need you."

She smiled. "Right back at you," she said, leaning up to kiss him tenderly. Slowly and meaningfully, their lips pressed gently in sensuous seduction, as the kiss gained a whole new meaning. Passion had been ignited and the fervor of wanting more began. She pressed her tongue to his mouth and he opened. She led, he followed.

When the kiss ended, he looked into her eyes, knowing without a doubt that he had released his past, because now he saw only his future with her. "Brice asked me today if I liked his mommy." She nodded, remembering the exchange. "I told him that I did, that I loved his mommy. It occurred to me that I never told you. I love you."

Her heart beat faster. It was filled with more than

she'd ever imagined. She reached up and kissed him. He wrapped his arms around her and held her tight as she melted into his embrace. This was where she wanted to be, in his arms forever.

As their lips parted he looked at her lovingly. "I should go," he said.

She shook her head. "You should stay."

"Natalia…"

"Make love to me," she whispered.

"But the boys are…" he cautioned.

"The boys are just fine," she assured him while caressing his face. Smiling, she kissed him again, then took his hand and led him upstairs to her bedroom. She walked him over to her bed and with her hand planted on his chest, sat him down then stood between his legs.

He took her hips and pulled her even closer. With their eyes fixed on each other, he slowly pulled the front zipper of her top down, opening her blue sleeveless sweater and revealing her skimpy lace bra. His eyes lit up with sparkling delight at the sight of his treasure. He pulled the sweater free from her shoulders and tossed it on the bench at the end of the bed. She moved closer still. Her lace-covered breasts met his line of vision exactly. She watched as he licked his lips and smiled wantonly. "Looks like you want something," she whispered seductively. He nodded slowly.

Without a second thought, a wayward boldness inflamed her passion. She leaned in, pressing the tips of the lace to his mouth. He opened his mouth and licked the scant material. The sensation of his tongue tasting her nipple sent burning ice through her body. She shivered and arched more, giving him exactly what he wanted. She rested her hands on his shoulders as he nibbled and tantalized the lace while holding her waist secure.

Slowly, she leaned back even more. His mouth puckered, trying to get the last lick. Trembling slighting from his assault, she began unbuttoning his shirt. Each button took particular focus as his hands began moving up her bare legs beneath her flared skirt. When she finished, she removed the shirt, tossing it on top of her sweater. She gazed at him with pleasure. His chest was magnificently toned with tight firm muscles rippling down to his stomach. His arms were tightly knotted with thick bicep and tricep muscles. She ran her hands over his chest and arms, feeling the solid power of his strength.

She took a step back and took his hand for him to stand up. He did. With deliberate agility, she allowed herself the pleasure of touching him. Her hands surged and flowed, teasing him to madness. His guttural groans increased as her nails etched across his burning skin, leaving tantalizing marks of pleasure. She boldly unbuckled the belt and unzipped the front of his pants. They fell to the floor. The bulge of his desire called out to her. She touched and caressed and gently scratched the length of him, raking her nails and finding his pleasure points. His body shuddered and his jaw tightened with steadfast restraint. She smiled, liking the power she wielded over him.

She leaned in and licked his nipple. Then she nibbled and licked mercilessly, sending his body through a myriad of rapturous longings. He grabbed her arms and held tight to still her. The dam was breaking. It was his turn.

Mastering the moment, he captured her face and leaned in, kissing her hungrily and fiercely. Mouth to neck to shoulder then back again, he kissed her in a frenzied trail of lust. His hands touched, kneaded and teased—both mindless and focused. The unrestrained passion set her body on fire. He was everywhere, all over her, all through her. Then he slowed to loving tenderness. He kissed her. His tongue dipped into her mouth, dancing with hers. Near breathless, she moaned, feeling the all-encompassing caress of his mouth. Then gently he again rained kisses down her neck to her shoulders and down the front of her body. He kissed, nibbled and licked the lace bra as he sat down on the side of the bed and unsnapped the front clasp.

The weight of her breasts opened the bra instantly, but didn't release it completely. He buried his face between the sweet swell of her breasts and tenderly kissed them. Natalia quivered as a surge of excitement took hold of her. Watching him, seeing his mouth on her, was intoxicating. Her legs felt weak and every nerve in her body tingled. Slowly, he nudged the lace apart, freeing her breasts for his pleasure. He pulled it down from her shoulders and immediately captured a nipple in his mouth. He suckled, sending shock wave after shock wave through her body. He licked her with the flat of his tongue then held their full weight and devoured her fully. She moaned, dropping her head back and biting her lower lip. Then he pressed both breasts together; taking them both into his mouth at once, he devoured her.

Breathless, she leaned forward to hold and stroke his face. He looked up into her eyes as she leaned down to kiss him. Eyes closed, heart pounding, she was entrenched in the pleasure he gave her. He reached around to the skirt's waistband. Finding the zipper, he pulled it down and released her skirt. It dropped to the floor and she stood before him in panties, pearls and heels. David looked down the length of her body and nodded his delight. She was breathtaking and she was all his.

Natalia watched as he encircled her breasts with his hands, then pressed his thumbs to her already hardened nipples, causing her body to quake uncontrollably. The stimulation was mind-blowing and it appeared that he was nowhere near finished with her. He stood, took her hands and raised them above her head. "Hold on," he whispered into her ear. She nodded, grabbed hold of the canopy's top and held tight as he moved all around her body, caressing, kneading and touching her freely. He trailed torturous kisses and maddening nibbles down her stomach and around the elastic waistband and then to her core. His mouth was hot and her body was on fire as kisses rained down all over her.

With labored breathing she gripped the wooden post above her head tighter as he moved to stand behind her. He reached up, feeling her hands on the posts. Slowly he drew his hands down the length of her arms to her neck. He kissed her shoulders then moved his lips down her arms to her thighs. He knelt down and caressed her rear, gently rounding her cheeks with the palms of his hands. His touch was like molten lava, melting her skin with each stroke.

The sensuous intensity of his actions made her writhe with desire. Standing became nearly impossible. He pressed close. She felt his hardened penis behind her. As he continued kissing her, he circled to cover her breasts again as he tantalized her nipples between his fingers and the palms of his hands. She sizzled and moaned. She released the post and reached back to wrap her hands around his neck. Holding on to him, she closed her eyes and dropped her head back as his assault continued. Kissing her neck and shoulders, she covered his hands on her breasts with her own. Then, as the space between their bodies vanished, they began to move in a syncopated rhythm.

Seconds later she turned. He held tight to her waist as he ravaged her body again. His body was already hard and now the sight of her nearly sent him over the edge. All he could think about was the feeling of being deep inside her, burrowing in and out, deeper and deeper.

She crawled onto the bed then crooked her finger, motioning for him to join her. He did. She lay back as he removed the last barrier between them. He looked down the length of her naked body and smiled. "You are so beautiful," he whispered, "but we're gonna have to be creative because I don't have condoms."

"I do." She reached over into her nightstand drawer and pulled out several small packets, smiling. "A hopeful gift from my sisters."

"Remind me to thank them one of these days." She nodded as his mouth, hot and wanting, clamped onto hers and his hand slipped between their bodies. He traced a burning trail over her breasts, down her stomach then between her legs. The mindless kisses did little to distract her from the pleasure he was giving her. He toyed with and teased her, sending wave after wave of rapture through her body. She dug her nails into his shoulders, holding tight as she felt her body soaring. With relentless zeal he took her beyond the point of wanting. She wrapped her arms around his neck, drawing him even closer. She moaned her pleasure, reeling from his actions. Her thoughts spun wildly, caught up in the whirlwind of ecstasy. He was fierce and gentle and bold and tender all at the same time.

"Now, David, now," she whispered into his ear. "I need to feel you inside me." She lay back, taking him with her as he positioned himself above her. He rose up to look down at her. His smile was placid and focused. Anticipation raced through her body as he hovered close, but still so far. She raised her hips, feeling his hardness at her entrance. David pressed down into her. She gasped as he filled her—thick, hard and long. Her body shuddered.

He rocked his hips into her, pulling in and out slowly. She echoed the rhythm he set. Together they moved as one, sending blinding streaks of ecstasy through their bodies. Natalia's arms held as her hands roamed over his back. The tempo increased as desire unfolded and unrestrained passion surged. Each vigorous thrust stoked the fire that ravaged them. The pace intensified, and he plunged deeper and deeper. She took him readily, over and over again, climbing higher and higher.

The building rapture swelled as they bumped hips faster. Then, slowing, they reset the pace, only to go faster still. He groaned, she moaned. She gasped, once, twice, holding her breath each time as he continued to enter her, all of him, tip to base. Then one last press swept them up in a swelled surge that plunged them over the peak. They erupted. Rapturous pleasure streaked through their bodies. Both went rigid as fulfilled climactic orgasms washed over them.

Sated and breathless, he collapsed to lie on top of her for a brief instant, then moved beside her, wrapping her in his arms and holding her tight. Her mouth was swollen from kisses and her body was weakened and wasted. Flushed with the heat of their lovemaking, she closed her eyes and snuggled closer.

Natalia laid her head on David's shoulder and inhaled the spicy scent of his cologne. She savored the sensation of being in his arms. For a brief moment the wish that this would last forever danced through her head. But she knew better. It was what it was, a sweet diversion and a lovely memory, a cherished keepsake to recall again and again. Instinctively, she cuddled closer. She sighed heavily, knowing that he'd be leaving soon.

"Natalia," he spoke softly. She took a deep breath, humming her response. "I love you," he whispered with a gentle kiss to her temple. She looked up into his eyes. They sparkled with sincerity and adoration. He nodded, smiling assuredly. "I love you with all my heart. In you I've found everything I ever wanted and needed. I love you, I'm in love with you, everything about you—your body, your mind and your spirit, your heart."

She smiled, speechless, as tears threatened to emerge. "David…"

"No, there is no reasoning and this isn't some kind of afterglow declaration. There is only feeling. This is real, as real as it gets. My heart is full, bursting with love, and you're the reason why."

"David," she began again as tears filled her eyes, "you don't love me. You can't. We don't even know each other."

"You're wrong," he said.

"It's the family thing," she reasoned. "Tonight, us, together, me and my boys, you were swept up in the feeling of closeness, family and love. It makes sense."

"I'm sorry, sweetheart, but you're wrong. I'm in love with you, Natalia Coles." He stroked her shoulder and arm lovingly as he smiled happily. "I can't stop this feeling. It's joy and fullness. Every part of my heart feels it, knows it. I can't deny it and you can't rationalize it away. It just is. If you don't love me right now, that's fine. I'll be patient, but know that only you can make me turn away, nothing else."

"David, I…"

"Shh, no, don't say anything right now. I just wanted you to know how I feel. Just be here with me and know that I intend to be with you for as long as you'll have me."

Natalia closed her eyes and snuggled close as tears fell. She was overjoyed and apprehensive and thrilled and scared and most of all in love. She wanted to say so much, but she couldn't respond. Not because he asked her not to, but because she was scared to. Natalia knew she loved him, too, and she wanted to wrap her arms around him and tell him. But he wasn't just an ordinary guy; he was famous and his world could turn hers upside down.

David looked down, sensing Natalia's stillness. She

had fallen asleep in his arms just as Brice had done earlier that evening. He drew a deep breath. Natalia was his and the boys were part of him. That was it. He closed his eyes and listened to the slow rhythm of her breathing and the steady beat of her heart against his chest. He stroked the length of her back and held her closer. He wasn't willing to let them go—ever. This was his family and it was going to last a lifetime.

Chapter 14

The next morning most signs of the heavy downpour the night before were gone. Tree limbs, leaves and scattered debris littered the already dried streets, but other than that, there was nothing. The sky was bright and blue, the sun shone brilliantly and the air smelled fresh and clean. It was like a new day, and a new chance.

The energy of the morning stoked David. He'd taken one last look at his sons before leaving Natalia's house. Now all he could think about was starting each morning for the rest of his life just like this one, making love to Natalia and then saying good morning to his boys. He felt a renewed sense of purpose. His life was in balance and he sensed that he was finally on the right path.

Work was one thing, but now he had found his center, a single point from which to draw strength, a family. It was admittedly something he'd avoided since his sister died. He strolled through the hotel lobby ten feet tall.

Fans asked for autographs and photos and he willingly obliged. In his current mood, nothing could derail him.

Moments later he burst into the suite, still swinging on cloud nine. He was so excited and emotionally charged that he felt as if his body was going to explode from sheer joy. "Pam, Pam," he called out as soon as he walked in. "Pamela."

"I'm right here," she said, looking up from sitting on the sofa with a pile of scripts around her. "Chill," she said. "What's wrong now?"

"Are you kidding? Nothing's wrong. Everything's perfect."

She looked at him strangely. "You're jolly?"

He chuckled. "Yeah, I guess I am. I met them and they're incredible. I need you to go shopping right now, this morning. I'm not sure what they need, so I guess we'd better just get everything you can think of— bicycles, helmets, skates, balls, lots and lots of balls, footballs, basketballs, games, computers, everything. Oh, and for Jayden, let's see, umm, you'd better get a catalogue. We'll just check off what we need from it. What's the name of that kids' toy store Lenny goes to all the time in Manhattan and Las Vegas?"

"FAO Schwarz?"

"Yeah, that's the one. Call them. Have a catalogue sent over this morning. And don't forget clothes. I don't know the sizes, so we'll have to guess." Pamela didn't move. Instead, she looked at him as if he'd gone crazy. "What? What's wrong? You're not moving and you're looking at me like I lost my mind," he asked.

"Ya think?" she said sarcastically. "Are you kidding?

You haven't smiled in over a week. Then you go out for one night and you come back a different man? Lost your mind, yeah. I'm leaning that way."

"I wasn't that bad."

"Guess again. Last week when you were away you were grouchy, short-tempered and downright mean. You snapped at a reporter, fired your publicist and made his assistant cry. You asked her when she was due. Duh, she wasn't pregnant."

"Hire them back," he said. "Send…"

"I already did," she interrupted. "And I also sent his assistant on a weeklong vacation to a spa in New Mexico to de-stress. Now, what's going on?"

He smiled happily. "I have two sons," David said, smiling from ear to ear. "You need to see them, Pam. They're great—well-mannered, funny, joyful and handsome. Brice—he's the oldest—he's a natural comedian. He's three years old and he's hysterical. He's always into something. Two weeks ago he caused a riot at the nursery school he attends. You're gonna love this story.

"Apparently, he didn't want to take a nap like all the other kids, so he stood up on his cot and started jumping up and down and calling out, 'No nap, no nap.' Pretty soon the rest of the kids followed suit." David started laughing. "Can you imagine that sight—three- and four-year-olds all jumping on cots in protest?" He laughed again.

"And then there's Jayden. He's handsome. He has light eyes just like Brenda's. He's quiet like her, too, but when he gets going there's no stopping him. He says 'Dada' and does belly laughs when you make faces at him. He's ten months old and he crawls, cruises and even tries to walk. I looked it up—he's advanced for his age. I can't believe it. I have two sons," he said proudly as he walked over to the suite's refrigerator and grabbed a bottle of water.

"No, David, you don't." He turned and looked at her, confused by her comment. "David, you don't have two sons. Natalia Coles has two sons." She handed him a folded paper. "This letter came special delivery yesterday."

David looked at it with suspicion. "What is it?" He took it and quickly read it over.

"It's from your attorneys. They did exactly what you wanted them to do. According to the clinic, the judge and your attorneys, you have no formal commitment and/or legal attachment to Brice and Jayden Coles. You're free, just like you wanted to be."

David read the words as Pamela said them. His heart slammed into his chest. This was wrong. "No, wait, what?"

"It's what you've wanted for the last two months, remember? It's the whole reason we came down here in the first place. You wanted to legally sever any ties between you and your biological offspring and to make sure that Natalia Coles wasn't going to be a threat."

"She's no threat," he said.

"I know," Pamela agreed.

David sat down heavily, realizing that the process he had set in motion weeks ago had now undermined his deepest desire. This wasn't what he wanted now. Fear and suspicion had blinded him. He had been cynical and skeptical of everyone. Being used by his mother and his family had a way of reinforcing that belief. But there were truly good people who wanted nothing more than to see others happy. Natalia was one of those people.

She had single-handedly changed what and how he thought. He took another sip of his water then shook his head while staring straight ahead. "I grew up without a father, I grew up poor, we had nothing, most times not even love," he began, seeming to talk to himself. "There was no role model for me to emulate, no one to go to when I needed someone, no one to say, 'Good job, son.' I'll be damned if I'm going to allow my sons to go through the same thing. Not if I have anything to say about it."

"David," Pam said slowly, "that's just it. You don't have anything to say about it. Technically, you're not listed as the father on the birth certificates. You have no rights, no obligations. It's what you wanted, remember?"

He looked at her. "You saw the birth certificates? Whose name is listed?"

"Apparently, there's a special classification and notation on the certificate. The father is listed as 'None.'"

"I'll have it changed. I want my family together, living with me in L.A."

"I don't see how. 'Cause it's not about what you want this time, David. It's about what's best for them. They don't even know you."

"They'll know me," he said defensively. "In time."

"After just one day?" she asked. "A few hours?"

"They will know me," he affirmed.

"You always said that you didn't want kids, and

particularly kids growing up privileged in the L.A. spotlight like the ones you've seen. How are you going to keep them out of all that?"

"Other actors have done it. I can, too."

"Sure they do it. Unfortunately, fifteen years later the kids are doing their third stint in rehab," she said. He looked at her, frowning. "I'm just saying what you already know. You know that scene—drugs, alcohol, pills and partying."

"I know what you're saying, and I agree. It will be difficult. But I'm sure we can do it. We'll live here in Key West."

"We?"

"Natalia and I," he clarified. "I told her that I loved her last night and I do. I love her with every fiber of my being. She's everything I've always wanted and much, much more."

"I know. I believe you. I see it. I've never seen you so happy and content. When you come back from being with her you're a different man and I'm truly happy for you, David. But you're not seeing the big picture." Pam shook her head. "Do you think she's just going to ante up and share her sons with you just like that?"

"No, of course not. I need to gain her trust. I'm doing that."

"News flash: You love her, but she doesn't have a clue why you're really here. You're not exactly scoring high points in the 'love and trust me' column."

"I need to talk to my attorney. I need him to petition the court for joint custody today, right now."

"You can't get custody for children you don't legally have a connection with," she said, motioning to the letter he'd tossed on the coffee table. "She's gonna think that you only want her for the children. How do you think that's gonna make her feel?"

He sighed heavily, facing facts as he paused to consider his options. There were none. "Is it true that time heals all wounds?"

"That's what they say."

"And that trust is the cornerstone of love?"

She nodded. "It's also true that hell hath no fury like a woman scorned and that a mother's protective nature can move mountains and that…"

"All right, all right, I get the point."

"There's nothing you can do now. What's done is done," she said. He didn't reply. She watched his expression change from desperate determination to doubtful despair. She hated to be the voice of reason, but someone had to be. "I'm sorry, David." He didn't reply. He just continued staring straight ahead. "Are you okay?" she asked. After a few seconds he nodded slowly.

"I still need to see Natalia." He stood quickly and headed to the door. An instant later he was in the hall, jabbing the elevator button.

"Wait. No, you can't," she stammered, grabbing the newspaper on the desk and following quickly, "Beck's here." David turned. She nodded. "I saw him last night. He was in the hotel lobby. Chances are he's still hanging out down there."

"I didn't see him downstairs just now when I came in," David said, remembering the other tabloid reporters taking his photo and asking questions, along with a few fans.

"Trust me. He's here." She handed him the newspaper and pointed out a specific article. "Either he knows everything or he's pretty damn close."

David started reading quickly. "This seems to have touched off the run on the L.A. sperm bank," Pam said. "Beck wrote an article about your going there. That's why women started camping out. Apparently, the story we concocted about visiting the clinic to research for an upcoming role didn't fly." David took the newspaper and read the article. The article was incorrect, but it sounded plausible enough that readers might think it was grounded in truth. "Obviously, the employees at the clinic have a different meaning of the word *confidentiality* than the rest of the world."

"Apparently."

"Beck's the best, and I hear that he offers nice incentives," Pam said, looking over his shoulder. "It's no wonder that someone talked."

"You're right. He is close, too close," David said. "I have to leave. I need to talk to Natalia right now. If he's this close she needs to know what's about to happen. If Beck is half the reporter I think he is, he'll figure this out in no time. That makes Nat and the boys an open target."

"Okay, I get all that. But you have a career to focus on, too. There are other things happening that need your attention. You've always been focused on your career, so if he sees that you're not now, he's gonna get even more suspicious. You've been canceling and putting some of these things off for days. If you keep ignoring them, it's going to draw attention that something's up, right?"

He paused a moment. She had a point. He nodded. "You're right," he said. "What else is going on?"

Pamela touched the screen of her PDA and brought it back to life. "Okay, you have two interviews scheduled today. One is in about fifteen minutes. It's a radio call-in, so you're okay time-wise. Your newly rehired publicist needs to speak with you about some publicity shots and the *GQ* magazine cover shoot can't wait. Campbell Barnett is directing a new film and wants to talk to you about the lead role as soon as possible. Your last film is ready to go to looping. Lenny has the revised contract for you to sign off on. Speaking of which, the script rewrites arrived last night. You're scheduled to make the talk-show rounds next week for advance promotions. Finally, the production team is teleconferencing this morning at nine o'clock their time."

"Is that it?" he asked. She nodded. "Okay, I'll take care of all that. I need you to get in touch with Beck. I want to meet with him. If he wants a story, I have one for him."

"You can't be serious. Since when are you so trusting of a tabloid reporter?" she asked.

"Since now," he said, smiling happily. "Also, I need you to get in touch with my attorneys in New York and set up a closed meeting. I need to make some changes as soon as possible. Have Lenny and my publicist there, too," he said, heading back into the suite. She nodded, already dialing phone numbers.

"And now you're a boundless optimist, too?" she asked.

"Falling in love has a way of doing that," he replied simply.

Pamela nodded, knowing that there was definitely something different about him. It had been a long time. She'd never seen him so centered and calm. Since Brenda's death he'd been harboring pain, but it seemed that the pain was finally gone.

"You know you can't take her to court to get your sons. The publicity would void the contract you're about to sign with the studio, not to mention kill your career."

"I have no intention of taking her to court. I do, however, have every intention of making her mine. Does Booker still work with Harry Winston on Rodeo Drive?" he asked. She nodded. "Get him on the line. I have a special order for him," he said as he dialed Natalia's phone number.

Brice dashed across the yard at full speed as soon as Natalia opened the back door. He headed straight for the play set her brothers had put together two years earlier. Natalia followed, carrying a picnic basket and a portable playpen. Niki, carrying Jayden, brought up the rear. Jayden, determined and frustrated, squealed and wiggled, eager to get down and follow his big brother to the play set. "Whoa, whoa, whoa, little buddy, you can't run over there like that," Niki said, holding Jayden tighter.

"You can put him in his swing," Natalia said, motioning to the small swing set placed beside the picnic area. Niki nodded, placed Jayden in his swing and cranked the handle. They walked over to the picnic table, and Natalia put down a tablecloth as they continued their conversation.

"This is what I wanted you to see. You're gonna love it. It came yesterday," Natalia said, handing Nikita an envelope.

Nikita opened the envelope and pulled out the letter. She read it quickly, frowned and then looked up at her sister. "What is this? The letter states they think that you want child support from Brice and Jayden's sperm donor?"

Natalia nodded. "I know, right. Can you believe it? How insane is that? The whole idea of me going through the in vitro fertilization process was not to deal with baby daddy drama."

"You know what? They probably sent this out to every patient involved in the in vitro fertilization process."

"Maybe, it just seems strange," Natalia said skeptically.

"You know how a lot of people are sue-happy these days. I'm sure that the clinic's attorneys are just covering themselves ahead of time, in case something like that happens."

"Maybe," Natalia said as Nikita handed the letter back.

"Okay now, getting back to our previous discussion—famous, wealthy, yeah, I get that part, but since when do you do the whole reckless abandon thing and since when do you fall for the gorgeous tortured type?" Nikita asked.

"Since said gorgeous tortured type is David Montgomery and I didn't just fall for him," she said slowly.

Nikita looked at her sister, seeing the expression in her face. "Natalia, you didn't."

"I did."

"Nat…"

"Niki, don't. I know exactly what you're gonna say, and believe me, I've had every one of those conversations in my head. It's crazy, I know it."

"That's not what I was going to say. I was going to ask you if you're sure and not just blinded by all the glitz and glamour of his lifestyle. I mean, do you know what you're doing?"

She shook her head and smiled. "I don't have a clue. For the first time in my life I'm not thinking straight, and that scares me. I'm going on pure instinct and feeling. It's insane to get involved with someone like him—I know it. I'm probably setting myself up for pain and heartache—I know that, too. He's a movie star and I'm a mom. Talk about a mismatch. But when he told me that he was in love with me I just…"

"Whoa, hold it, back up. He told you that he was in love with you? When?" Nikita asked.

"Last night. He stayed over. I can't believe I did that. You know I never have men stay the night when my boys are here. Anyway, I'd promised the boys a picnic after work, but then it stormed and so we had the picnic in the den. After the boys fell asleep, David stayed. We made love and he told me that he was in love with me. Nikita, the man is absolutely wonderful. He's everything I ever wanted. Being with him is like living for the first time. Don't get me wrong. I was happy before and my life was complete before, but now there's even more. I don't know how to explain it."

"You don't have to. Look at you—you're positively glowing. You have stars in your eyes, literally. But what happened to Ms. Practical and Forever Level-headed?"

"I know I said it was supposed to be a simple tryst. But it turned into something much more. I'm in love with him."

"Be careful, Nat. Things aren't always what they seem and neither are people. You know he'll be leaving eventually, right?"

"Of course I know. I've been with enough jerks and have had my heart broken enough. But with David it's different. Yeah, I know he's an actor and his job is to make you believe the characters he plays, but I see more. I feel more."

"You do look happy," Nikita said.

"I am. I'm very happy," Natalia said. "I've asked myself how I could possibly have feelings for a man I hardly know."

Nikita shrugged. "You can't."

"But I can't help it. I feel what I feel. My heart won't listen to my head."

Nikita smiled. "Excellent. It's about time. I'm so happy for you, girl."

"You don't think I'm crazy to feel this way."

Nikita laughed. "Yes, of course I think you're crazy. But that's what love is. It's irrational, illogical and unfair. It's also blissful and, yes, it's even a little crazy." She reached out and hugged her sister. "Be happy and enjoy the ride. It might get bumpy, but I'm sure it's well worth it."

"That's just it. I don't know that it is. It's not just my heart, it's the boys, too. You know how attached they get to people. I can't do this to them."

"You're hiding behind motherhood, Natalia."

"No, I know that eventually it's going to be over. I'd rather be the one to choose the time and place. That way I have some control over this."

"Wait, you're ending it? Nat, the man said that he was in love with you. Didn't you believe him?"

"Yes, that's what makes it so hard. But I can't live in his world and what about Brice and Jayden? Can you really see them as Hollywood kids? Paparazzi, red carpets, mansions—the whole thing is too over the top. It's not me. I'm a realist, we can't work this out. I know I need to end it."

"But maybe…"

"Niki, trust me. It'll be for the best."

"When are you going to do it?"

"David's out of town right now, so as soon as he gets back."

"Love, real love doesn't come around that often, Nat. Are you sure you need to do this?"

Natalia nodded, knowing that Niki was right. Love was all those things. And right now she was feeling everything. She watched her boys playing in the yard. This was her life, plain and simple. And the reality was that there was no way David could be happy here. He was too used to his world. And there was no way that she could live in his world. One taste of Miami showed her that.

Ultimately, she was fooling herself. It was physical. It was sex. They had enjoyed each other's bodies and for a brief moment she had the attention of one of the most famous men in the world. She had to end it for both of them.

"I sure know how to pick 'em," Natalia said.

"Yep, you sure do," Nikita replied. "But I have a feeling that it'll all work out in the end." At Natalia's skeptical look, she said, "It will. Just be open to love."

Chapter 15

Deliriously, ecstatically happy was an understatement, but it didn't matter. David had said that he was in love with her—that didn't matter, either. He had called her ten times a day to tell her that he loved her and missed her. She missed him and that mattered. But loving him and fitting their lives together were two different things.

He'd been gone for two days and there was a gaping hole in her heart. Natalia dropped down on the sofa with both Brice and Jayden in her arms. She sat Jayden down beside her and helped Brice off with his book bag. Brice talked nonstop about nursery school and everything he'd done that day. Natalia listened, smiling and asking questions to keep him engaged. It was a usual evening. She cooked dinner, they ate, took baths, she read to them and then tucked them in and stayed with them until they fell asleep.

Then alone, she turned on the fireplace, went into her

home office and continued working on finding funding for the center. As soon as she sat down, the phone rang. She answered.

"Ms. Natalia Coles."

"Speaking."

"Ms. Coles, my name is Claire Pitts. I'm a senior laboratory director and I'm calling from ABM IVF Clinic in Los Angeles. As you well know, we appreciate your patronage. Our successful services are our utmost concern. We take a multitude of precautions with all security procedures. Our security protocols are beyond measure and we take great pains to keep the chain of custody intact and uncompromised."

"Exactly what is this about?" Natalia asked.

"It has recently come to our attention that your file and information have been illegally compromised."

"Excuse me?" she asked.

"An employee, a laboratory embryologist, has divulged your personal information to someone outside this facility. Please be assured that the most severe and suitable penalty has been levied. The employee no longer works for this company and has been databased and redlined to all nationally working clinics as asserted by the rules of the College of American Pathologists. Effectively blackballed."

"You're saying someone looked through my file from the clinic and gave the information to someone else?"

"Yes."

"Why?"

"We're not sure."

"How is that possible? How did it happen?" she asked.

"We don't know at this point."

"Why? Why would someone even care about my file?"

"We're not sure."

"Are you sure of anything other than the fact that someone out there knows that I have two sons who were conceived via in vitro?"

"Ms. Coles, I'm afraid it's more specific than that. It appears that your information and the information of the donor have both been compromised."

"The donor, as in the sperm donor?" she asked.

"Yes, I'm afraid so."

Natalia went blank as a noiseless vacuum seemed to surround her. If the lab director continued talking, she had no idea what she said. She'd stopped listening. All she could think about was the safety of her children. She hurried to their bedroom with the phone at her ear. They were both sound asleep in the toddler bed and crib. She walked over and touched each forehead and smiled. They were safe.

Finally, tuning back in to the woman on the other end of the line, she heard her mention something about the donor's attorney. "Wait, what are you saying?"

"Our attorneys are looking into it."

"I purchased the sperm outright. It belongs to me."

"Yes, but as I just said, there's a problem since that particular sample wasn't supposed to be offered to anyone."

"So you made the mistake of selling me a sample that wasn't for sale."

"Yes, it appears so. In cases like this, the donor and client usually come to an accord with the assistance of the facility. We've contacted the donor and he wishes to have a relationship with his offspring."

"What? No! He has no right to my sons. He's their biological father, but he's never had a relationship with them."

"We understand your feelings, Ms. Coles, but if you could…"

"What part of *no* did you not understand?" she asked.

"We know that this is a very difficult time for you and we are grievously sorry for your inconvenience…"

"My inconvenience—are you kidding? There's some man out there who wants to know my two sons for no reason other than that he's a sperm donor. You call that an inconvenience?"

"Ma'am…"

"No, no, it's not going to happen."

"Ma'am, the donor wishes to meet with you. Our clinic will, of course, provide counseling and an arbitrator to facilitate the meeting."

"No."

"We can…"

"How can this be happening?" Natalia muttered to herself.

"We will facilitate everything at your convenience."

"No."

"Ms. Coles, this situation is extremely rare, and please know that our legal department is all over this. There is no known official legal precedent, but we're willing to yield to whatever both you and the donor suggest and agree to."

"There will be no compliance. The answer is no. I will not meet with this man. I just received a document from an attorney confirming that all paternal ties have been legally relinquished. Not that there should have been any in the first place."

"I understand and again, we are extremely sorry for this terrible mix-up." She continued talking, but again Natalia stopped listening. All she could think about was a strange man being with her sons. The thought physically sickened her. The doorbell rang and she realized that the woman on the other end was still talking and stating her case. "I need to go."

"Yes, of course, but please consider my suggestion— just one arbitrated meeting. I'll give you some time to process this. We'll contact you again in a few days. Thank you for your time and, again, please know that we are extremely sorry about this situation." The doorbell rang again. Natalia looked toward the living room, but still didn't move. "We are willing to do whatever it will take to resolve this amicably for both you and the donor. Good evening."

Natalia nodded, remotely hearing the buzzing sound of the disconnected line. She released a breath she seemed to have been holding since she first picked up the phone. Her heart was pounding and her hands were shaking. She couldn't breathe. Her doorbell rang again. She walked over slowly and opened it. David stood smiling at her. She lurched into his arms. He dropped the small bag he'd been carrying. "David, you're back."

He hugged her tight, smiling at the joy of feeling her in his arms again. He wasn't sure how long this feeling would last. He closed his eyes and prayed that it would last forever. He'd come to talk, to tell her the truth, the whole truth—everything. He'd talked to his attorneys and to the clinic. "Let's go inside," he said softly, still holding her close. "We need to talk."

She sighed. "I don't want to talk. I want to feel." She kissed him hard, hoping his strength would somehow bolster her own. She wasn't sure what would happen next, but she knew that she would fight whoever this donor was for the rest of her life. "Make love to me."

"Natalia, we need to talk. I need to…" He stopped midsentence, seeing the pain and fear in her eyes. His heart suddenly froze and then galloped like a charging horse. "What is it? What happened? What's wrong?" he asked. "The boys—Brice, Jayden—are they okay? Where are they?" he stammered.

"They're asleep."

"What is it? What happened?"

"I don't know. I think I'm in trouble."

"I'll take care of it—whatever it is. Don't worry," he said confidently.

"No, you can't. If this goes public, I don't want you anywhere around me."

"What are you talking about?"

"I was going to end our relationship when you came back anyway. One of us has to stop living this fantasy. This merely adds to all the reasons why I should. Make love to me now, David," she repeated.

"No, Natalia, not like this. You're upset and vulnerable," he said, backing away. "I can't take advantage of you."

"Are you saying that you don't want me?" she asked thickly.

He almost choked at the absurdity of her statement. His body was instantly hard the second she opened the door. "Sweetheart, right now I want you so badly my body could cut diamonds. But I can't do this to you, to us."

"Why not?" she asked.

"Because it's wrong."

"No, it's not," she said, kissing him repeatedly. He closed his eyes as a deep, wounded groan pulled from his throat. She pressed closer, feeling him already thick, full and hard for her. "You want me?" She pulled the hem of her shirt up and over her head. "Right here, right now."

David looked away—she was killing him. He knew he had to tell her the truth, but he couldn't. How did he tell the woman he loved that everything they'd been to each other since the moment they'd met was a lie? "We need to talk," he said.

"No, I need to feel you inside me. Make love to me, David, one last time." She unzipped her skirt and let it fall to the carpet. His breath caught, leaving him speechless. She reached behind and released the bra's hooks. It loosened and then fell on top of the shirt and skirt.

He knew this could very well be the last time they would ever be together. That thought tore him up inside. As soon as she knew the truth, everything he felt and everything he'd grown to love would be gone.

She pulled at his shirt, ripping the buttons, then tugged at his pants. Unzipping them, she instantly felt what she wanted and needed. He grabbed her hands to hold her still. "Natalia, you know that I want you. I've always wanted you. The first moment I saw you in your office I wanted you. Then getting to know you only made me want you more. But I want all of you now and forever. If we make love, you will hate me and hate yourself."

"No," she said weakly.

"Yes," he said, nodding. "Believe me, you will, and I can't do that to you. Hate me, fine, but not yourself and not what we have together. But know that I love you with all my heart. Do you believe that?" he asked. She nodded ardently as her tears continued to fall. "And I love our sons. They are the most precious gift a man could have and you did that for me." She nodded again, not really listening to his words. "I love you."

Natalia's tears flowed and overflowed. Hearing his words and knowing in the deepest recesses of her heart how much he loved her made her want his love even more. She pulled at his pants again. This time he let her. Seconds later they stood free from restraints, baring everything. He took her into his arms knowing that it was the last time, but praying that it was the beginning of their life together. "I love you," he whispered as he gently brought her down to the sofa. "I love you."

"I love you," Natalia said, pulling him to lie on top of her. Already wet and ready, she guided him to enter her and the smooth ease of his body instantly filled her with joy. They made slow, patient, enduring love, each already feeling the loss of a lifetime together. He entered her, grinding his hips, pressing exactly where he knew she'd receive the most pleasure. This was for her. It was his gift for everything she'd given him, his life back.

Natalia refused to close her eyes, no matter how good she was feeling. She wanted to see everything, feel everything. David had shown her how to love and trust again. She knew that she could never hurt him. But being with him after this would do just that. When everything about the clinic came out, as she was sure it would, she wanted him as far away from her as possible. She needed to protect him and his career.

Their love continued to flow, then in an instant of sheer ecstasy, they released all the tension and pain in orgasmic pleasure. Moments later, they lay in each other's arms, each in silence and thoughtful of the other. David leaned up, knowing what he had to do. "We need to talk," he said, staring at her.

"I don't want to talk," she said. "Not now."

"I've run out of time."

"You're leaving?" she asked as her heart jumped.

"No, never. I'll be here in the city for as long as it takes for you to forgive me."

"Forgive you for what?" she asked, suddenly nervous.

"Natalia, it's me. I'm the donor."

"What?"

"Brice and Jayden are my biological sons."

Her heart froze. "You?" she asked. He nodded. "What?"

"The clinic sold what wasn't theirs to sell. When I found out, I was livid. I never wanted children. I never wanted anyone to grow up as I did. The only reason I donated sperm was to get the money to go to New

York for a career move. I'd forgotten all about it. Then I received a letter of apology from the clinic telling me about the mixup. I needed to know who you were and what your intentions were."

"That first day we met," she began, and he nodded. "You thought I knew about you, didn't you? That's why you wanted to give me a check and no publicity. You were paying me off to keep quiet."

"I wasn't sure what you knew or if you'd gotten the same letter and intended to use it as blackmail or something."

She nodded. "I didn't know."

"Yes, I realized that later."

"When?" she asked.

"That day at the café, the second time, outside."

"We only met at the café once."

"Twice. I saw you and your sister, but neither of you noticed me."

"The man with the newspaper at the next table," she said. He nodded. "You were listening to us." He nodded again. "So you knew when I went to your suite."

"Yes."

"And you still didn't say anything?"

"No."

"Why? I don't get it. Why pretend that you were interested in my center and the kids? Why keep pretending? What, were you—bored and in need of a distraction before your next movie started filming? So everything after that was just you playing, honing your skills?"

"No. You of all people know better than that."

"No, I don't. How could I? I don't even know you."

"You know me, Natalia."

"Yeah, right, sex. I guess that was all just fun and games, too—everything leading up to your taking my boys."

"No, never. You're an incredible mother. I would never…"

"Save it for the Oscars when it really counts. We're through here."

"Natalia…"

"What? What could you possibly say to me that would change my mind?" Her eyes blazed with hurt, pain and love. "How could you play with my heart like that?"

"I never played with your heart. The thing is, I lost my own in loving you. I couldn't stop seeing you even if I wanted to."

"Why are you telling me this now?"

"There's a tabloid reporter, Beck. He's here in Key West. He's very good at what he does. He will find you and the boys. Say whatever you want, I'll back you up."

"You need to leave," she said.

He nodded his understanding. "I had everything a man could want or ask for—fame, money, everything that didn't really matter. But still I wasn't happy. Then I came here and found you. Yes, I know I was wrong. But I do care about the center and the kids there. They're just like I was. And I do love you—that you can't deny. In the end it all boils down to what's missing. You, my family, you're what's missing in my life, just as much as I'm what's missing in yours. I came to ask you to be my wife, to marry me."

"Is that your solution to all this?" she asked.

"No, it's my hope, my dream, my prayer." He walked over and picked up the bag he'd dropped when she first opened the door. He took out a small ring box. He opened it, got down on his knees and placed it on the coffee table in front of her. "Natalia, please, look at me."

"I can't."

He nodded. "I cherish you with all my soul, I adore you with all my spirit and I love you with all my heart. Please Natalia, be my wife." She didn't respond or turn around.

He walked to the front door then paused. "I'm not giving up on us, Natalia. I can't stop loving you. I don't even know how and I wouldn't even if I could. I do know that every moment and every second that we were together was worth the pain in my heart right now." He closed the door behind him.

She just lowered her head and closed her eyes.

Chapter 16

Two days passed, then another two days and another two days. Natalia walked around in a trance, devoid of feeling and emotion. She went about her daily life, but everyone saw that her heart wasn't in it. The L.A. clinic had called twice. David had called only once after she'd had his ring delivered back to him. He stayed in the suite, walking around just as miserable. The last call from the clinic was from their attorney's office. They informed her that a place and time had been set up for arbitration. To expedite matters they had set it up almost immediately and in Key West.

Natalia arrived early. David did, too. He opened the door and walked inside. "Ah, excellent. You're early, as well. Mr. Montgomery, Ms. Coles, my name is Kirk Claymont. I'll be arbitrating these proceedings. Please have a seat here, Mr. Montgomery, and we'll get started." David took a seat across the table from Natalia, staring intently at the table the whole time. When he sat down, Natalia looked at him as if she didn't know him. His heart sank. "I'll assume you both know the particulars of this meeting, so I'll disregard the usual procedure. This arbitration will not be recorded, in agreement with both parties."

Claymont looked from Natalia's face to David's. They stared at each other; their expressions were the same. He cleared his throat and opened a folder, preparing to begin.

"Mr. Claymont, would you please give Ms. Coles and myself a moment alone."

Claymont looked at Natalia. She nodded her agreement. He stood and hurried out the door, sparing one last look before leaving.

"Hello," he said.

"David," she responded.

"I hoped you would come. Thank you."

"I'm here strictly for business. Whatever happens here today will impact my sons for the rest of their lives. I need to think of them first and foremost."

He nodded his agreement. "I agree, and I will consent to whatever you want. But if you want me to leave and not come back…" He trailed off, unable to finish the sentence. "Nat, I know you're afraid of this, of us. We started all wrong and that was my fault. We happened too fast, but that doesn't make what we feel any less real. I know that you're not just protecting Brice and Jayden, you're protecting yourself. Nat, stop hiding behind motherhood. This, me, I'm here for you. I know that you've seen so much family pain in your work, but do you know real happiness when you see it, when you have it?"

She looked at him. Her heart was breaking. She knew he was right about her. She was afraid.

"I'm here for you. All you have to do is say yes."

"And if I want you to leave?" she asked.

His heart lurched. "I can't abandon my family. I will not be my father and my mother. You mend hearts and create families. Here's your chance for love and a family for yourself."

She understood his implication. He was right. Her job was to ease suffering and complete families. But she was too afraid to help herself to his love and complete her own family. She stood and walked to the large windows. Looking down at the street, she saw a gathering of people waiting at the front door. "Paparazzi are everywhere."

"I know."

"Your career will probably take a major hit if any of this comes out."

"I don't care about my career. I care about my family."

She turned; her eyes were deadly focused on him. "The center received a donation by way of an anonymous bank check a week ago. You wouldn't happen to know anything about that, would you?"

"The center does good work," he said. "You do good work. I saw no reason why it shouldn't continue. And before you ask, no, you didn't win my foundation's grant. I got together with my attorneys to set up a special awards program. The Teen Dream Center happened to be the first award recipient."

She nodded slowly. "Are you trying to buy me?"

"No, I know full well that I can't."

"Did you ever intend to take my sons from me?"

"No, never. That was never my intent," he said forcefully. "I started all this to find out what kind of woman you were. What kind of woman was raising my children. I was afraid you were like my mother, uncaring and selfish. Then spending time with you banished my fears. I realized that you were exactly the woman I wanted in my life, too. It was you—your qualities like loyalty, integrity, honesty and selflessness."

"Tell me one thing: Was any of this ever real? Bimini, Miami, the boat, any of it?"

"Yes, everything. My feelings were and are very real." He stood and walked over to her. He thought about when she'd said that their son had had an accident. The feeling in his gut had been completely foreign to him. He'd been shaken and disturbed, and no amount of emotional detachment could change that. Knowing that his own flesh and blood was injured pained him. He feared reliving that pain again. Walking away now would incur that same kind of pain, but he'd do it to save them all.

Slowly she turned and looked up at him. She shook her head. "I'm so off balance with you. I don't know how I feel. I'm angry, I'm hurt, I'm fearful, I'm a shattered mess and I'm..." She paused.

David smiled, knowing what she was going to say. "That's funny, because you make me feel the exact opposite. With you everything is clear and calm. Suddenly I know what I want in my life. I want you. Please honor me and be my wife."

"I can't live in L.A."

"We won't."

"Your world is— I can't be a Hollywood mama."

"You could never be."

"My life here is insulated. Yours is a media circus. Reporters are everywhere. It's crazy. Nothing will ever be normal."

"Then we'll create our own normal."

"I need to protect the boys from this tsunami."

"*We* will protect the boys," he assured her.

"I do want you to be a part of my son's lives, our son's lives," she said.

"And your life?" he asked hopefully.

She nodded. "Yes, and my life, too."

David smiled and tipped her chin to his mouth. "May I?" he asked.

"Yes," she said as his mouth came down onto hers. The kisses were sweet and lasting. When they ended she smiled, breathless, almost in tears. "I'm afraid to close my eyes or to even blink. If I do, all this will disappear."

"I won't let it," he whispered in her ear.

"I never thought I'd want this, but I do."

"I like the way you say that," he replied.

"Say what?" she asked.

"'I do.'" He pulled out the box she had delivered back to him. He opened it and took the ring out. It sparkled and shone like a brilliant star pulled down from the night sky. He placed it on her finger. "Marry me."

She immediately felt shivers down her spine. "David…"

"No more questions, no more second thoughts, no

more fear. There's only yes. I'm in love with you, Natalia Coles, and I know in my heart that you're in love with me, too."

She nodded. There was no denying her feelings. She did love him. "Yes, I love you."

"Then there's only one thing to do." He released her and dropped to one knee. "I love you." Then, just as Brice had taught him, he crossed his heart with his finger. "I want to spend the rest of my life with you, and it isn't because you're not like other women I've dated or that you're a psychologist and social worker or that you're the mother of my children. It's because you make me deliriously happy. You fill me, you complete me. And spending another day without you in my life is unacceptable. I want to take you as my wife right now, today. Will you marry me now?"

Natalia's heart jumped as she struggled to catch her breath. She looked into his eyes. They were focused and clear and pleading for her answer. Protecting her heart was no longer an issue. She'd freely given it to him. Hiding behind motherhood was no longer a barrier. He was the father of her sons. Her heart wanted her to surrender. "I don't know what to say," she stammered.

He smiled. "This is where the cue-card person usually steps up to give you your line. But since it's just the two of us, say yes, you'll marry me." She nodded joyously. "Is that a yes?"

She nodded again while smiling through tears. "Yes, yes."

He grabbed her, picked her up and twirled her around. Then, placing her on the floor, he pulled her close and kissed her. When the kiss ended, she couldn't stop smiling. He took her hand. "Come on, we're gonna be late."

"What about the arbitration?" she asked.

"Don't worry about that. Come on—this way." He led her out the door down the hall to another door.

"Wait, what's going on?"

Pamela rushed out of the room. "Your attorneys have made all the arrangements and we're all set," she said, smiling. "Congratulations, welcome to the family." She dashed back into the room just as quickly and closed the door behind her.

"What was that about?" she asked.

"Marriage and adoption. You, Brice and Jayden will have my name and my love from now until forever."

"But don't you want a prenup or something?"

He laughed and kissed her quickly. "Forever," he reiterated.

"But…"

"But right now we're getting married," he said, kissing her again, this time more tenderly. "Come on, everybody's waiting for us."

Natalia's happy smile turned quickly to shock as she realized what he'd just said. "What? Married now? Right now?"

"Right now. You can plan any kind of wedding you want after this, but right now I can't go on another moment without your being my wife." He took her hand as he opened the door.

"Wait, what does that mean?"

The applause struck her instantly. Her family, her friends, everybody stood smiling as they walked in. Seeing everybody smiling and happy, she looked at the man by her side. "You were pretty sure of yourself, weren't you?"

"I was," he stopped and corrected himself. "I *am* very, very sure of us and our future together. Happy Mother's Day, sweetheart." Natalia was too overjoyed to speak, but she did cross her heart with her finger. David crossed his heart, too.

A robed judge stood at a desk and nodded. He motioned them forward. David led Natalia to the front. She saw Nikita and Tatiana each holding Jayden and Brice. Her brothers, her mother and father, Mia and Stephen held each other closer, smiling happily. Moments later David and Natalia stood before the judge and exchanged vows. Their whirlwind life of forever was only just beginning.

* * * * *

The fourteenth novel
in her bestselling
Hideaway series...

**National
Bestselling Author**

ROCHELLE ALERS

NATIONAL BESTSELLING AUTHOR

ROCHELLE ALERS

Desire always finds a way...

Breakaway

A HIDEAWAY NOVEL

Recovering from a trauma at work, E.R. doctor Celia Cole-Thomas escapes to her remote cabin on the Tennessee border. There she isolates herself from the world—until FBI agent Gavin Faulkner moves into a nearby lodge.

As soon as he meets her, Gavin is determined to show Celia the passion she's been missing—but his dangerous assignment could shatter the trust they've built...unless he can convince her that love is worth the risk.

*Coming the first week of May 2010
wherever books are sold.*

ARABESQUE®

**www.kimanipress.com
www.myspace.com/kimanipress**

KPRA1820510

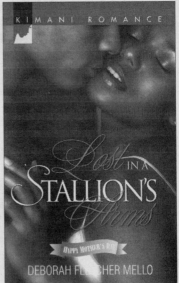